PURR-FECT GETAWAY

A Wonder Cats Mystery Book 5

HARPER LIN

ISBN-13: 978-1987859331

ISBN-10: 1987859332

www.harperlin.com

CONTENTS

About the Author

Broken Heart

❦

"We just hate to see you this way, Cath," Aunt Astrid said.

I guessed she didn't appreciate my new grunge-style look—baggy sweatpants and the same hoodie I had been wearing for no longer than six days. I could have sworn it hadn't been a week. Surely not.

"I'm *fine*." I smiled as if I was trying to expel a kidney stone. What else was I going to say?

The truth was that every time I opened my mouth to speak, tears rushed to my eyes. I'd bite my tongue until the urge to cry passed, looking away as if some dust bunny on the floor was suddenly the most important issue in life.

"Honey, I say this with love: you are starting to

stink." My aunt's tone sounded gentle, but the message was harsh.

I had been in the kitchen most of the day with Kevin Baker, our baker. He'd needed some of the twenty-pound bags of flour moved, and I'd changed a light bulb over the stove. Plus I had helped take down all the Halloween decorations and pack them back up in the storage room, which was in desperate need of organizing. I raised my arm, took a whiff, and within a nanosecond regretted that idea.

"I showered yesterday," I grumbled as I continued sweeping the floor. The café was closed. My cousin Bea had already left for the day, so it was just my aunt and me locking up.

Aunt Astrid looked at me with her right eyebrow arched, her arms folded across her chest, and the same "you're not fooling me" kind of look detectives gave suspects during intense interrogations. I was pretty sure she wasn't believing anything I said.

"Cath, that house in Prestwick took a chunk out of all of us."

I blinked and jolted back as if I had gotten slapped. That house in Prestwick with its nightmare visions and tentacled monster and horrid little children that weren't children at all but something much more sinister—that house took more than a chunk out of me.

I chewed on my lower lip. I wanted to say something to my aunt, but I found no words.

"Please, Cath, let Bea help you."

"Aunt Astrid, I told you already. I'm fine."

Her psychic ability might have been showing her a vision of me driving off a cliff or drowning in the river. Perhaps she could see in me the fight I'd put up at that house in Prestwick to save Blake Samberg before help had arrived.

I could tell she saw something by the way her eyes bounced all over me. Those intense blue marbles of hers barely looked directly into my eyes. She was watching something, and I wasn't at all interested in knowing what it was. Nor did I want my empathic cousin to lay her hands on me. For the first time in my life, I just wanted to deal with this like a regular person.

She took a step toward me with her arms open. I wondered if I would have backed up and put my hands up defensively if it were my own mother trying to hug me.

I brought the broomstick in front of me like a shield.

"I just want to be alone. That's all. I don't have to clear that with everyone, do I?"

The words came out with more anger than I'd intended, but I was kind of glad they did. It drove the point home, and my aunt let her arms fall to her sides.

"No. Of course you don't," Aunt Astrid sighed.

"Okay. Then let me finish cleaning up so I can go home. I just need some rest."

With slumped shoulders and tired eyes, Aunt Astrid reluctantly nodded and turned back toward the counter. She finished with the receipts, stuffing them into a big green canvas pouch, and shut the register drawer with a ping.

"You'll lock up?" she said almost as if my locking up the café was the saddest event to take place in Wonder Falls in a decade.

Without looking at her, I nodded and mumbled "yes" while still sweeping.

She walked to the door without saying another word. I had my back to her, sweeping as if it was a chore I loved and couldn't get enough of. I heard the deadbolt clunk, the door pull open and set off the tinkling bells, and then a solid thud. She was gone. I was alone.

I took a deep breath and finished sweeping. I

wiped off the counter and did three dishes that hadn't gotten washed. After snapping off the lights, I pulled out my keys and stood there for a moment in the darkness.

Through the café's front windows, I saw a couple walking across the street. I heard the woman laugh out loud at something her date said then lean her head affectionately against his shoulder.

Finally, they passed out of view. I took the seat my aunt usually occupied during business hours. I didn't want anyone walking by to peek in and see me. The little table for two next to the counter was concealed almost completely in darkness.

In the dark, I could feel all the little nicks and scratches its surface had accumulated from being used so much. I liked the feeling of being in the dark, unseen by everyone but still able to watch the world as it went by. It wasn't like the solitude of being in my own home. I used to enjoy being there, but now it felt more like a cage than a home.

Sleep wouldn't come at nighttime no matter what I did to make myself tired. I had cleaned the entire house from top to bottom, sweeping out cobwebs and getting rid of things that had overstayed their welcome, like clothes I didn't wear anymore or books I'd never read again. Still, as my body creaked with relief when I lay down, my mind would keep reeling, skirting the big ball of haunted house that seemed to reside right there in the middle of it.

I let out a breath that I hadn't even realized I had been holding. Then I started to cry. If I were to tell the truth to anyone, something inside me was broken. A light had gone out, and I had no idea how to fix it.

I wasn't sure how long I sat there in the empty café. Maybe I was there twenty minutes or maybe an hour. When you are lost, time becomes very difficult to gauge. Direction is even worse, and I was afraid I had lost my direction.

My cousin Bea just wanted to help. That was her shtick. Throughout our life together, there really wasn't much we didn't share. Bea was my cousin, my sister, my best friend in the whole world. Normally, if I had an issue, I'd run to her to talk it out.

But now the thought of doing that made me wrinkle my nose in disgust. Her help felt like pity. Bea had everything. In addition to her nice home, she had a husband who accepted her "gift," the healing ability passed along to her through the Greenstone bloodline. Jake was even in awe of it now. Plus, Bea was just a good-hearted person. She was beautiful and smart and kind in a way that looked a person right in the eye, making it clear she never wanted anything in return.

Her goodness was too much. How could I tell her that? How could I tell my cousin and best friend that I didn't want to see her right now because she had what I wanted? If I did go over to her house like she had been begging me to do for the past couple of weeks, I stood a very good chance of running into Detective Samberg.

Blake and Jake. Partners on the police force were like old married couples. Already Blake was making himself comfortable at their house on a fairly regular basis. He was the last person I wanted to bump into. Just the thought of that happening made my heart crack open.

Technically, we were never dating. We'd barely exchanged three civil words to each other over the past several months. In fact, ever since we'd met, he had been a prickly burr in my side.

But we had staked out the Roy house together, and I knew it wasn't just me. A spark was there, one of those brief, intense jolts that suddenly made you see a person differently, maybe romantically.

Then there was the Prestwick house. I protected him. I risked my life for him. Didn't that mean anything? Didn't *I* mean anything? Obviously I did not, because he was dating Darla now.

Part of me wanted to hate Darla Castellan even more, if that was possible. All those years I turned the other cheek to her bullying in high school, all the times I bit my tongue when my family was around, all the times I held back ... holding back seemed like the dumbest move since General Custer decided to crash Little Big Horn.

Sadly, another part of me thought, *What's the use?* Darla couldn't help that she was pretty and rich and knew how to fit in with all the right people. It just came naturally for her. I was just a square peg in a round hole, and I would be the same with or without Darla. It made hating her feel like running on a treadmill: a lot of work that got me nowhere.

While I held my head in my hands, I saw the shape of my aunt appear in the doorway. She tapped lightly on the glass, knowing full well that I was sitting there feeling sorry for myself. Hastily I wiped my eyes and shuffled to the door to unlock it, leaving the lights off.

"I was just getting ready to lock up," I lied.

"I'm so glad you are still here. I forgot my reading glasses, and you know I'm as blind as a bat without them. But I need them to read, and if I can't read before I go to bed, I'll never fall asleep." She hurried behind the counter, apparently knowing exactly where she had left them. "Um, Bea has made dinner tonight. Vegetable fajitas with cornbread and refried beans. You want to stop by and we'll fix you a plate? You don't have to stay."

The first words that came into my head were *hell no*. I went to the table where I had been sitting and pushed in the chair. "No thanks."

"Are you sure? I think she's got some chocolate cake for dessert."

"I just want to go home, Aunt Astrid. Please let me do that."

"Bea really misses you. You barely talk to her when you're working together, honey." My aunt's eyes were hard. Getting to the bottom of things was what she was trying to do, but that would be impossible since I felt like I was still falling. The bottom was a long way off. "Just talk to her. It might help. It can't hurt."

It can't? I thought bitterly. It can't hurt to say, *I'm tired, sick of being a Greenstone, and wish this witch's curse could be lifted off me forever so I could just be normal?* Bea would never understand. *I* don't even understand. I don't know where these thoughts are coming from, but they are in my head, burning my mind and making me cry when I'm alone in the dark.

Looking at my aunt's face, I was convinced that I'd better lie. "I will. Just not tonight. I'm tired."

"Okay, honey. Maybe tomorrow."

"Maybe," I said, trying hard to smile in the semi-darkness but hiding from the light from the street-lamp so my aunt couldn't see my face that clearly.

That must have sounded acceptable, because Aunt Astrid started going on about something, I don't know for sure what, about her neighbors and some raccoon or something, to which I nodded and agreed when I thought it was appropriate. Who knew what she was saying? She could have been asking me if I wanted a severe case of poison ivy with a twist of hiccups for good measure. There I was *yeah, sure, yes*-ing all over the place.

Finally, we both stepped outside into the cool autumn air. My bulky set of keys rattled as I locked up the front door.

The idea of being away from the Brew-Ha-Ha Café for the next several hours sounded good. Just two short weeks ago, I'd loved coming to work. It hadn't felt like work at all. I'd joke with my family and chit-chat with the regulars, and even the hard-est, most undesirable chores weren't bad because the boss was family. It wasn't brain surgery, but I did love it.

Tonight, I was happy to go home.

"Okay, see you tomorrow," I chimed, trying to sound optimistic. Giving my aunt a quick peck on the cheek.

"It won't feel like this forever, Cath. I promise," she whispered as if sharing a secret no one else should hear.

Did she mean the broken heart over that jerk Blake, or did she mean the weariness of being a Greenstone witch?

I nodded, stuffed my hands into the pockets of my hoodie, and hurried in the direction of home.

Rattlesnake

✿

"Cath, we have a bit of a situation here. Can you please talk to this rattlesnake that's decided to make itself at home in Jake's car?" Bea asked over the phone before I left for work at the café. "He left the door open last night because his hands were full with groceries. Poor thing just climbed in the back seat where a nice square of sunshine had heated up the leather. Jake nearly had an episode when he saw it. Scared the hell out of himself and the snake." She laughed. "Now he's— the snake, I mean—hiding under the seat. None of us dare reach under there to get him or even peek at him with him being a rattler and all. Poor thing is scared, I'm sure."

Without letting the annoyance come into my voice, I agreed to help. What else could I do? As lousy as I was feeling, I couldn't let my family handle a rattlesnake when I knew full well I could coax it out safely and quickly without even touching it.

I walked out of my house and down the street and saw Bea and my aunt standing on one side of the car and Jake on the other. All I wanted was to get this done quick before Blake showed up to ride to work with Jake.

"Thanks, Cath," Jake said bashfully.

"No problem," I mumbled, smiling a little. I pulled the door open and looked into the back seat. I saw nothing there.

"Uh, he scooted under the passenger seat. You better get in there a little and see. Hop up on the seat till you can get a bead on where he's at."

"*It's okay,*" I said in my head to the snake. "*You don't have to be scared. Everyone has gotten out of the way especially for you.*"

No answer.

"*Really, no one is going to hurt you. Why don't you let me see you?*"

Still nothing.

I climbed slowly and carefully into the back seat, pulling my legs up tightly underneath me. Then the door swung shut.

Before I knew what was happening, Bea had run

around the car and hopped into the driver's seat. Aunt Astrid was in the passenger seat. I was trapped by child safety locks in the back seat.

"Thanks, honey," Bea said, rolling down her window to exchange a big kiss with Jake.

"No problem," he told her. Then he looked at me. "Try and have a good time, Cath. They're doing this for you."

My aunt Astrid and cousin Bea were giggling, peeling out of the driveway like hillbillies at a monster truck rally.

"What the hell is this?" I whined, pulling my legs out from underneath me.

"Just what you need," Bea replied happily. "We know what's wrong with you."

"Oh really?" I snapped. My mouth didn't curve into a sly smile. My eyes didn't twinkle. Instead, I glowered at my cousin in the rearview mirror.

"You're overworked," my aunt chimed in.

"Stressed," Bea added.

"Overwhelmed."

"Pissed!" I interjected.

They both let out groans. "Uh-oh, someone woke up too early today." Bea laughed again. "Now you just relax back there. In one hour, we'll be at the

Muskox Serenity Spa and Retreat Center. It's just what you need."

"We all need it," Aunt Astrid said, paying absolutely no attention to my temper tantrum.

I shook my head, folded my arms over my chest, grumbled sarcastic remarks that barely made any sense, and even cursed.

"It's no use, Cath. You're going. And if you don't feel better after a deep tissue massage and a pedicure, we've got a padded room reserved for you at Bellevue."

"Why don't you just take me there now?" I squawked. I knew I was being childish, but I couldn't help it. "I don't know how I could have fallen for something so stupid. You two should be aware that this is technically kidnapping." I felt as if an invisible dunce cap had been placed on my head.

"Cath, we tried to be nice about it," Bea said, still smiling. When I saw her eyes twinkling, I felt she was making fun of me. She had shaken off the magic burnout from the Prestwick house in less than forty-eight hours, and my aunt had suffered from it only slightly longer. But I was still trying to shake it. The fatigue had settled in my bones like arthritis.

"Wait!" I yelled. "What about Treacle? You guys

didn't even think of him. Who's going to feed him and—"

"Jake promised to check in on him, or pick him up at Old Murray's if he winds up at the animal shelter. He's also already locked up your house and will be checking in on it every day. That's one of the perks of being married to a member of the Wonder Falls Police Department."

Was that a dig, I wondered. Was Bea bragging just then?

"What about the café? Who's going to run that? Kevin can't bake and run the front. My gosh, he'll slash both wrists during the morning rush hour."

"Kevin is getting four paid days off. You won't hear a peep of complaining out of him," Aunt Astrid said without looking back at me.

I scooted my right leg underneath me again and looked back out the window. I was still in the sweats I had slept in, which weren't much different from the ones I was wearing to work these days.

"What about my clothes?" I said, suddenly feeling like an ugly duckling between two swans.

"We already arranged to have new clothes there waiting for you. And you'll be happy. They are yoga clothes. Not quite the Rocky Balboa sweat suits you've been wearing, but I promise they'll be just as comfortable," Bea said, pushing a long red lock away from her face.

It was no use. These two witches had thought of everything. I wasn't going anywhere but to Muskox Serenity Spa and Retreat Center.

Well, I had one last card to play: I could pout. I did for the entire hour we were in the car. I barely spoke and didn't make eye contact. Since I was miserable, I was determined to make them miserable as well. It wasn't like me to do that or to behave this way. But I hadn't been feeling like myself for a long time.

Muskox Serenity Spa

❧

The silence in the car was refreshing. Unlike the chatter and busyness of the café at this time of morning, the hum of the engine and slight bumps over cracks and potholes in the road had a soothing effect.

I had heard of the Muskox Serenity Spa and Retreat Center. It was situated just a little more than an hour away from the center of Wonder Falls. It was in an unincorporated part of the town, so things were sort of mismatched and jumbled when it came to the city agencies. Wonder Falls Police Department handled all their emergency calls, but they got their garbage picked up by the WM Waste Management Company of the next town over.

The patchwork district realignments were obviously the genius ideas of a couple of decades' worth of politicians trying to reinvent the wheel. The retreat center had been built a long time ago and had been renovated, adding a spa and salon, within the past fifty-five years.

The traffic to get there was always heavy, with lots of semi-trucks and views of the concrete barriers blocking out the scenery. But Muskox Serenity Spa recommended a little longer, less travelled route, promoting it as starting your spa experience before you even checked in.

That was the way Bea decided to take. She slipped in a CD of smooth, mellow sounds that reminded me of birds chirping and water trickling over rocks.

Reluctantly, I did manage to get lost in the view. The autumn leaves had almost all fallen from the trees, leaving a tapestry of bare gray limbs among dark patches of maroon, purple, and dark-green foliage. Little white flowers dotted the ground. Majestic hawks circled overhead, their wings holding steady as they silently glided along the breeze in search of prey. The steep cliffs, low hollers, and hills made it look like one of those paintings by that guy with the afro hairstyle who painted beautiful nature scenes in a half-hour television show.

I cracked the window and inhaled the cool, fresh

air. My head felt like a heavy blanket was finally being pulled off of it, and my muscles started to tingle as if I had been holding heavy books in my arms and finally set them down.

The distraction came in the form of a deer carcass lying off to the side of the road. I saw a herd of about a dozen deer, their heads up proudly, watching us as we drove past the field they were in. It happens, right? Deer try to get across the road only to get caught in headlights or taken by surprise, and they freeze. But then I saw another carcass. And another. I counted six before we reached the billboard pointing us up a black, paved, private road to the spa.

Unless the deer population had boomed up here, I found the number of bodies to be unusually high. Something inside me twisted, and my shoulders shook with shivers.

"They have natural hot springs here," Bea said.

I felt no need to say anything. A part of me wanted to make my relatives know I was still angry over being abducted. The chip on my shoulder had not receded.

But as we pulled slowly up the winding road to the spa entrance, I couldn't hide my surprise. The building was constructed of honey-colored wood and cream-colored brick. The thick beams gave it a rustic feel, yet it oozed elegance, with elaborately beveled glass windows that had to capture hundreds of rainbows every afternoon when the sun shone in.

The parking lot was cobblestoned. As we pulled in, we saw magnificent urns holding seasonal foliage that draped languidly over the edges, spilling out like leafy tongues in rust, evergreen, and fuzzy gray tones.

We stepped out of the car—me last because Aunt Astrid had to open the rear door from the outside thanks to the child safety locks—and felt the shift in the air.

"This will be good for all of us," Bea said. I saw my aunt looking around, seeing more than Bea and I did. Her eyes were gathering all kinds of information from this astral plane as well as from two or three more.

Bea stretched and rubbed her arms against the cool air. She hopped to the back of the car, happily pulling two overnight bags out of the trunk and slinging them over her shoulders with no effort at all. Like a little kid who had seen how many presents were under the Christmas tree, she happily helped out in order to get to the goodies that much sooner.

"This is going to be a blast," she said to me, bumping me with her hip.

"This is more beautiful than the pictures on the web," Aunt Astrid said.

I wasn't ready to give up my attitude and grumbled "I guess." I wanted to be excited. I wanted to join my cousin and aunt in their enthusiasm and run inside like a little kid looking for the indoor pool during a winter holiday, but I couldn't. Something wouldn't let me.

Bea tried to take my hand in hers, but the feeling of her warm touch made me pull away. She looked at me as if I had just called her a rude name.

"You're going to feel better. I promise," she said quietly.

I blinked and shrugged, and we headed inside.

The lobby was even more beautiful than the exterior. Chihuly glass sculptures hung from the ceilings. Mosaic tiles covered the floor. For an instant, my heart jumped into my throat as I remembered the living tiles from the Prestwick house. Were these the same? Were they cursed? Destined to start writhing and pulsating under my feet? No. They stayed still in a simple pattern like the cobblestones out in the parking lot.

My breath began to slow down before I even realized I was starting to hyperventilate. A cold sweat was ready to cover my skin but only succeeded in dampening the areas under my arms, making them feel cold and uncomfortable.

"I'm going to go sit down," I whispered to Bea.

"You okay?" she asked, her eyes clear and healthy. I felt like I was looking through a sickly yellow film at her.

"I wish everyone would quit asking me that," I griped and walked over to a small loveseat next to the concierge desk. Flopping down, I felt as if I had run a marathon coming in from the parking lot. I'd sat in the car the whole time. How could I possibly be tired? It had to be the anxiety of being abducted from my own home under a ruse. Yeah. That was it.

"I don't want a free night," a male voice snapped. "I want a refund. You couldn't get me to stay another night in this place for all the tea in China, missy."

I leaned around the desk and saw the man speaking. At any other time, he probably blended into the scenery unnoticed. Average height with a slight spare tire around his midsection and a head that was shaved but gave away a horseshoe pattern of stubble, indicating he was balding and had decided to beat the inevitable to the punch.

"I do understand, Mr. Kline. You were in room

116," the desk clerk said patiently. Tapping away on her keyboard with French-manicured nails, she barely looked at the man.

"I never saw such things," he mumbled, patting his shirt and pants, making sure he had everything he needed: wallet, keys. "Right out of the wallpaper it came. I thought this place was supposed to be for relaxation. I'm more stressed now than I ever was in the pit of the New York Stock Exchange in the days of paper and pencil, I'll tell you that much." He wiped his forehead.

"I understand, Mr. Kline. Some of our guests do claim to experience some strange things."

"Strange things?" he said, almost laughing out loud. "No. Strange is when you know you shut the lights off before you left for dinner and come back to your room and they're on again. That's strange. Not having a pale woman come out of the wallpaper, screaming and running out of your room without opening the door. That is horrifying. *Horrifying*. Do you see the difference?"

The woman nodded while typing away. Finally a sheet of paper was spit out of the printer behind her. Ripping it off, she handed it to the terribly nervous Mr. Kline, who didn't even wait for her to explain his charges being refunded.

He grabbed the paper, picked up the suitcase at his feet, and stomped through the electric double doors and out of view. As I watched him, I noticed his shirt was partially untucked, his suitcase had the cord of a phone charger and another piece of clothing sticking out of it, and I could have sworn he didn't have any socks on. I wondered how long he had stayed before he decided to leave.

Truthfully, I was not as interested in the man's experience as I was in the clerk, who didn't seem to bat an eye at his story. Pulling myself up, much against the will of my cranky, screaming joints, I walked over to her.

"Excuse me," I said, feeling a headache start to settle at my temples. "I couldn't help but hear what that man was saying to you."

She looked up, flipping her black ponytail behind her and smiling in that plastic *How can I help you?* way.

"Um...is this place...you know...?"

"Haunted? Yes."

Haunted

•❀•

I t wasn't what I'd expected to hear. Suddenly my heart began to race like it had that time in high school when I realized I had forgotten my science report at home when it was worth half the semester grade and due that day.

I waited for her to continue, but she didn't say anything and just kept typing away on her keyboard.

"Well, what's the story?" I prodded, leaning on the counter half to support myself, half to get close enough for her to tell me the gory details.

"Let's just say the Muskox has a very rich history. I can't tell you any firsthand stories because I have not experienced anything myself."

"But what that man said about things coming out of the wallpaper, a woman? Was the guy just drunk, you think?"

Her eyes simmered. "We don't provide any alcoholic beverages here. This is a holistic spa, and everything from the lighting to the arrangement of the furniture to the food is meant to help bring healing to our guests."

This tennis match of words was not going anywhere.

"Okay. I didn't mean anything by it. And just because you don't provide the juice doesn't mean a person can't pack their own." Sure, I didn't need to be snarky about it. But neither did she, right? I flipped my own unbrushed, bed-headed hair behind me. "But if the place *is* haunted, I just wanted to know..."

Her voice was low and velvety. "Some people claim to have items move in their rooms. They claim to see a woman. Some people claim to see shadows. If you take a look, you can find all of this on our website if you click on the history tab. Like I said, personally, I haven't seen anything." She looked at me as if her eyelids had suddenly gotten heavy. "I'm sorry, but I've got to get ready for a bridal party that will be arriving. If you have any other questions, I can give you the name of the manager. He is not on duty right now but will be tonight around eleven."

"I'll probably be sleeping by then," I muttered,

clucking my tongue. "It's okay. Thanks anyways." I managed a smile and so did she. Not mortal enemies after all.

So this clerk hadn't seen anything. No mention was made of a tragedy surrounding a lover's triangle ending in murder. No missing child later discovered to have fallen to his death down a stairwell.

I looked up and saw Aunt Astrid and Bea smiling as they talked with the man behind the counter, who was giving them their keys and a little verbal tour of the place. Something he was telling them got two very enthusiastic nods, and they waved and thanked him as they walked away from the counter and toward me.

A rope pulled inside my gut. Should I tell my family this place was haunted or keep it to myself? If I told them, they might want to investigate. What would that mean for me? I wasn't sure I wanted any more of the paranormal in my life. But if I didn't tell them, I could be risking them getting hurt. Ghosties and ghoulies and creatures that creep have the tendency to seek out witches like them—like us.

The words wouldn't come even if I'd wanted them to. Quickly, my mind had dug a shallow hole and tossed the information into it, covering it with the dirt of a dozen other things, including anger. The small house I lived in just a few blocks from the Brew-Ha-Ha Café in the center of Wonder Falls was not haunted. It was safe. It was mine. I wanted to be there. Not at this place. This haunted place.

"Hey. We are all on the same floor," Bea said, handing me a plastic credit-card-sized key. It had a lotus flower on it. *How original,* I thought. "Cath, are you all right?"

The mental dirt I had just thrown on that little bit of information began to move as if something was trying to dig itself out. Hitting it hard with a mental shovel seemed to work for the time being.

"You know, I'm tired and hungry and still not altogether willing to be here," I said, pulling my hair back and looking down at the key in my hand. "A shower. Some breakfast. I'll be better." I managed a smile.

The word I really wanted to say didn't come out. It hung in my throat like a piece of dry toast. *Scared.* I was scared to be there. The idea of seeing something like I had at the Prestwick house loomed like a fast-approaching cliff.

The Muskox Serenity Spa and Retreat Center had three floors of beautiful rooms. We were on the third floor in room numbers 310, 318, and 323. I took the room closest to the fire escape, 323.

When I walked in, the whiteness was nearly blinding.

Even though the day outside had a light-gray ceiling of clouds, it could not stop me from gasping at the amazing view.

I slid open a thin glass door, letting the chilly air rush in. I stepped out onto a small balcony made for two lounge chairs and nothing else. The bare trees looked stoic, waiting for the colder weather and blankets of snow that would be arriving in a few more weeks. A body of water mirrored the sky off to the right, and I could see a sprinkling of boats floating on it. They were little black spots, and I wondered how chilly it must have been down there by the water.

Closer to the spa, I saw the steam rolling up from the natural hot springs. People lounged in them. They all looked very content, with their arms spread out to the sides, supporting them, as their heads leaned back in complete relaxation.

But it wasn't the people that caused me to stare and lean slightly over the balcony's edge. It was the movement I had suddenly noticed behind the springs. I watched for a moment, thinking a cat or a raccoon or something that size might be creeping behind the soakers. But just that quickly, it was gone.

A trick of the steam, I thought. That was what it was. Sure, animals were probably very used to humans walking through the trails and sitting in the springs. Food probably brought the critters much closer than they normally would have ventured. But it was just how the steam was rolling and billowing, like sheer curtains over an open window just before a storm.

Just before a storm. Why did those words echo in my head?

The wind kicked up and sent a chill over me that sent me back inside my room. It was pretty. And the bed looked very inviting, with a super-thick comforter, half a dozen pillows, and a faux-fur afghan at the foot.

A nap. That was all I needed. But before I could make that dream come true, a gentle knock sounded at the door. Exhaustion fell on me and weighed my shoulders down. What now?

"Just one last thing," Aunt Astrid whispered as she walked in, carrying three bags from the gift shop with pink tissue paper poking out of the tops. "Your wardrobe for the next three days."

I had almost forgotten that I had no change of clothes, and I managed a smile.

My aunt set the bags down on the little desk next to the three free postcards and pen with the spa name written on it.

"Take a shower. Eat something. Rest. Then come to meet us in the lobby around two." She kept her voice low as if a baby was sleeping in the room or a sick person was trying to get some rest. Wasn't that sort of the truth? She went to hug me but I stepped back, taking her hands in mine and shaking them in some moronic handshake.

"Okay," I said, making it painfully obvious I wanted to be alone.

I saw her eyes squint for just a brief second as if she was trying to see around me, behind me. I turned but saw nothing there. When I looked back at her, her face held its usual understanding expression.

Without another word or look, she turned and went to the door, stepped out, and let it slide shut behind her, the lock clicking into place with metallic finality.

No matter what was wrong with me, I had to admit getting some new clothes was exciting. I peeked into the first bag and saw lovely yoga pants in navy blue, gray, and rust colors. They had matching shirts and even some jewelry. Flip-flops. Headbands.

"Wow. They went all out," I mumbled. Then I saw the card. I pulled it out and opened it up to see a watercolor picture of some beautiful leafy vines growing up what could have been the side of a castle. The inside was blank except for the words written in Bea's elegant scrawl.

"We understand."

I shuddered and nearly collapsed where I was standing. My eyes flooded with tears, and the sobs raced from my throat, making my whole body jerk. I tried not to wail even though that was what I really wanted to do. Instead, I hobbled to the bed and let gravity pull me into the soft pillows and comforter.

Without anyone around, I let myself wallow in this sadness that seemed to completely envelop me, and I cried. It was that deep, guttural crying like I had done when the realization my mother was not coming back had hit me. She had been dragged underneath my bed by twisted, mangled, inhuman hands, and I'd never see her again. Except no one had died here. Or had I?

Burying my face deeper in the pillow, I mourned the part of myself that I thought was dying. My spirit was shriveling up like a fern deprived of water. I could feel my bones becoming brittle and dry. My heart, which used to pump with wild excitement when Halloween or my birthday with my family came or when I'd see...him, was slowing. Each beat was an epic, painful struggle, as if it wanted to just quit. How terrifying was that to even consider? That my mind wanted to keep going, but my heart wanted to just stop, to give up.

Once I thought I contained no more tears, I let myself fall asleep. I don't know how long I was out, but when I woke up, my eyes stung. I went to the bathroom. I hadn't even looked at it when I arrived and was surprised to see a white, lion-clawed tub with a handheld showerhead attached. Complimentary fizzy bath salts the size of tennis balls were stacked on the counter beside a sink that looked like nothing more than a glass bowl on a wooden pedestal.

I turned on the hot water, dropped in a fizzy, and watched as the water swirled around and the sweet smell of roses filled the air. As I watched, I had a flash of the Wonder Falls waterfall near the part of the river where my dear friend Min Parks and I had gone to talk and make plans when we were in high school. For a split second, I was there. I could smell the earth. I could feel the mist against my skin. The water.

And just like that, the image was gone. I climbed into the hot bath and washed my hair and face. Then I stayed there for a while until my fingers became like prunes and my cheeks were bright red.

Trick of the Light

꿏

By the time I finished soaking and got dressed in one of my new outfits, I was feeling a bit better. My muscles still ached as if I had gone up and down a bunch of steps a day or two ago. Perhaps I had done just that trying to keep busy and keep my mind off Blake Samburg. I couldn't be sure, but it wasn't totally out of the realm of possibility.

The clock next to the bed read 1:34 p.m. I was supposed to meet Aunt Astrid and Bea in the lobby at 2:00. I had just enough time to put on some of the jewelry they'd bought me. Brushing my hair and pulling it off my face into a tight ponytail felt good. I looked in the mirror and was surprised at what I saw. Staring back at me was a very feminine, soft-looking woman.

Was I pretty? Maybe a little. Certainly not like Bea, but in my own way, I thought I had some stuff, good stuff.

Just then came a knock on the door. Stepping into new flip-flops with little jewels dangling from them, I went to the door and pulled it open. Expecting to see Aunt Astrid or Bea, I smiled broadly and started to say "How do I look?" but no one was there. I stuck my head out and looked down the hallway, first to my left and then to my right, where it ended just a few feet away at the red EXIT sign and the heavy metal door leading to the fire escape.

I was hearing things. It was as simple as that. Letting the door pull itself shut, I was turning to go pick up my key from the nightstand when I heard something else. I froze, held my breath, and listened. Scratching. I heard scratching and a raspy female voice mumbling unintelligible words in a venomous tone. The sounds were on the other side of my door.

Images of those rotten little black-eyed children jumped into my mind so abruptly that I took a step back. It couldn't be them. No. But my mind wouldn't let me push their wicked little images aside.

For a second I contemplated jumping into the bed and pulling the comforter over my head. That would make me safe, right? That's why children were never harmed or saw their mothers pulled under their beds by monsters.

"Enough," I whispered. I tiptoed to the door and raised my hand to the knob, only to be humiliated by it trembling as if in an impersonation of Katherine Hepburn when she and her Parkinson's disease had reached the ripe old age of ninety.

I gripped the doorknob, took one big breath, held it, and yanked the door open. Nothing. No one was there.

"I heard it," I said to myself, only a second later realizing I had called the noise and female voice "it."

Shaking off the shiver that ran up my spine, I headed off down the hallway, tucking my card key into the breast pocket on my loose, flowy blouse. No one was in the hallway. No housekeepers were knocking on doors or mumbling crazily inside other rooms. No one could have knocked on my door, let alone stood scratching and panting outside it.

"I'm burnt out. That's all," I uttered out loud. "I can't do this anymore. That's all there is to it. The powers that be are telling me it's time to get out while it's not too late to have a normal life." The thought was painful, but I was sure it was true. I had lost my nerve.

As I headed downstairs, I wondered how I'd tell

Aunt Astrid and Bea about this. Maybe I wouldn't have to if I found another job, maybe sold the house and moved into a small condo in another town and made all new friends. Yeah, that would work. People were always trying to be my friend because of my sparkling personality. Even my thoughts grumbled those words. I was as approachable as a hungry feral cat and about as embraceable as a cactus.

Once down in the lobby, I looked around but didn't see my relatives anywhere. It was then that I realized I was getting tired again. I had slept all morning after my crying session. I should have felt refreshed, but instead I had this weird feeling that I was plastic wrap that had stuck to itself. Fresh air was all I needed.

I walked out the electronic sliding doors and let the hot sun chase the chills away. A slight breeze blew, but it did little more than carry some pollen and a lazy leaf or two down from a drying branch.

I exhaled and checked whether I could see my own breath. Not yet. It wasn't that cold. I rubbed my neck and stepped out of the way of the other guests coming and going. I found loads of fall flowers and foliage to study from where I stood on the sidewalk. It amazed me how much nature still seemed to be alive even as the season was winding down for its long winter nap.

It seemed no matter where I looked, I found a hidden treasure of a bright gazing ball perched among some pussywillows or a little wooden door at the base of a wide old tree or the bird feeders and bird baths that attracted bright yellow or blue winged creatures. Some bird zipped by every couple of seconds.

Fat, heavy bumblebees still bounced along the little white flowers. Bright-green things were still sprouting, literal late bloomers. I listened and heard trickling water that must have been coming from the hot springs. Maybe I'd find a waterfall around here, too.

The thought of that made me feel hopeful. Was this just a funk I was in? Would I wake up tomorrow and feel better? I doubted it. That had been my mantra over the past several weeks. Every day I went to bed saying *Tomorrow I'll feel better. I'll feel like myself.* And every day I woke up with that sinking feeling that nothing had changed.

But wasn't all this beauty, this nature, wasn't it all a sign that things could get better? The late-blooming plants and the fat bumblebees didn't know it was almost time to call it quits. They just kept going, right?

As if in a sick answer to a naïve question, I spied the pink innards of what had been a chipmunk not so long ago. It had been torn open, probably by a raccoon. Now ants and flies were making their way over and inside it. While I watched, three other chipmunks came out from underneath the decorative slabs of stone and began tugging on the body, one at the tail end, one at the head. I stared.

Why would they do this? Were they trying to eat the remains? Did they eat their own? I had never heard of such a thing in the rodent world. Not that I was all that privy to it. I watched in gruesome fascination as three figures buried their heads, side by side, in the exposed cavity. They were from the same family. I shuddered even though the sun was making me feel hot.

Hey! Stop that! What are you doing? Leave that alone! I called in my thoughts. Rodents were harder to communicate with than cats. It was like trying to have a conversation with someone who had extreme attention deficit disorder.

I listened but didn't hear anything except a weird humming coming from them. They were gone. Something else had taken over. Whether that was good, old-fashioned instinct or something more insidious, I couldn't say. I wrinkled my nose, shook my head, and stepped aside for a more tranquil view. But something inside kept prodding me as if I was meant to see that gross act of nature. Was it an omen? As a witch, I was supposed to believe in that sort of thing. I was supposed to take heed and let the rest of my coven know.

"But I don't want to be a witch anymore, right?" I grumbled to myself.

I looked off into the uneven barrier of trees only to gasp! What I saw there looked like a daddy longlegs spider that had grown to the size of a cat. I wouldn't have noticed it except that it shifted its position. It had moved when I spoke to the chipmunks.

"No," I muttered. It must be a trick of the light. But then a human-like head tilted up at me. It was a sickly white with large red eyes that pierced through the shadows from the overhead branches like the tracers of a scope on a rifle. It grinned.

I looked behind me to see if anyone else could see it too, but I was all alone. Funny how just seconds ago I had been musing to myself about all the life, all the activity in the woods, but when I turned toward the parking lot and entrance to the spa now, nothing moved. I could have been staring at a picture. I whipped back around and saw the tree again. No giant human-arachnid hybrid. No fiery eyes. All I saw now was a weird pattern in the tree bark. Just a regular tree that had probably been in this spot for over five decades.

"Just a trick of the light," I soothed myself. But a grumble began in the center of my chest and continued to grow. Seconds before a full-blown panic attack took over, I realized it was the roar of an approaching motorcycle that was causing my heart to dance inside my ribcage.

Tom Warner

❧

A limousine came chugging up the cobblestones to the front entrance just behind a police motorcycle. The cycle's red and blue lights were flashing. My first thought was that we were all going to get kicked out because some politician didn't want to risk bumping into the riff-raff that had actually voted him into office.

However, when the officer hopped off the bike and opened the door on the stretch, four lovely women carrying champagne glasses hopped out. The fifth woman to emerge had a short little white veil attached to her head. Then two much older, portly women brought up the rear. This had to be the bridal party the desk clerk had been talking about.

As all the women giggled and chatted their way inside, I couldn't help but envy them. They didn't see any creepy spider with a human head grinning at them.

It was just your imagination, Cath. That's all.

I tried to comfort myself and think of how nice it would be if I were to get married someday. If I were going to shed my witchy ways, perhaps that day would actually come.

The police officer stood for a moment before slamming the car door shut. He was facing me and looking at something. I turned around and saw nothing there, and when I turned back, the officer was smiling.

He was wearing sunglasses and looked very cool in his black boots and holster. Just as he gave me a wave, the young lady with the tiny veil came running back out. She said a few things to him, kissed him on the cheek, and then dashed back into the lobby.

Typical, I thought and turned back to face the woods. The wedding was probably tomorrow and he was going to try and get one last fling in before he had to give up the single life for good.

Back to focusing on the wildlife, I strained to see anything out of the ordinary. It had to have been a trick of the light, or I was just seeing things. Tired or confused or a little bit of both.

"Excuse me." The deep voice made me gasp as I

whipped around. It was the police officer. "I'm sorry. I didn't mean to sneak up on you."

He took off his sunglasses. His jaw was square and perfectly complemented his flattop haircut, which was so short that only his thick black eyebrows indicated what color his hair really was. Long black eyelashes framed blue eyes that seemed to dance like the water by the river at home did. His lips were thin and curved in a smile that produced a dimple in his left cheek.

"Do you happen to know what time it is? I think the battery in my watch just died."

"I think it's just about two. You could probably ask your fiancée and she'll tell you." The irritation in my voice was like sandpaper.

"Fiancée?" The puzzled look on his face was almost convincing. Then he rolled his eyes. "Ugh! That's my sister. The one with the veil, right? Yeah. She's my sister. She's getting married next week."

Folding my arms over my chest, I looked at him skeptically.

He didn't seem to be too put off by my incredulity and kept smiling.

"My name is Tom Warner." He stuck out his gloved hand. What could I do? I didn't have to be completely rude.

"Cath Greenstone," I said, taking his hand and shaking it.

"Greenstone. Are you related to Bea Williams?"

"She's my cousin. She's here too."

"I know her husband. He needed help from some of us state troopers for a sting operation a while back, and we got to spend a little time together. A real nice guy. Detective Jake Williams, right?"

"Yeah," I said, nodding, feeling the ice start to melt under the gaze of those blue eyes.

"Can't say the same for his partner. But Jake's a good guy."

That was all I needed to hear.

"So, you gave your sister a police escort? That was really sweet."

He smiled and looked at the ground for a minute.

"Yeah, it was just to give her a little thrill." He stood there for a moment as if he was waiting for something. I just enjoyed looking at him. He had the kind of shoulders that made you think if he really wanted to, he could just hoist a lady over one of them and carry her off into the sunset. "Are you here with your fiancé?"

I blushed and giggled like a lunatic.

"No. More like a little R&R with my aunt and Bea."

"No fiancé?"

I blushed a dozen shades of red and shook my head.

"Okay," he said, smiling as if he approved. "Well, Cath Greenstone. I have to get going. I've got to go to work in a couple hours. It was nice meeting you."

I took his hand again and smiled, too.

"What's that thing they used to say on that cop show on television? Let's be careful out there," I said, feeling corny but too late to stop it.

He smiled. I spied that dimple again.

"I remember that show. *Hill Street Blues*."

"Yeah. Is that what made you decide you wanted to be a cop?" I joked.

"No. It was *The Andy Griffith Show*. I wanted to be just like Barney."

As much as I didn't want to, I started to laugh.

"That's awesome," I replied, not sure what else to say.

He started to walk away and then stopped. He turned around to face me again.

"Jake Williams is a detective for the Wonder Falls PD, right?"

I nodded.

"That's great, because I live in Segal and do all my shopping in Wonder Falls."

"Well, maybe I'll see you around some time," I said, still smiling.

"I think you might." He turned, and I watched him as he walked back to his bike, climbed on, started the engine, slipped his sunglasses back on, and drove away. Sure, he was strutting a little, and yes, I'm sure he knew how sexy he looked riding that motorcycle, but I liked it all the same. I didn't expect to ever see him again. But for those few moments, I'd laughed a real laugh, and it felt good.

When I went back into the lobby, I saw my aunt and Bea waiting.

"Sorry," I said, shrugging. "I lost track of time out there just looking at the scenery."

"No worries, honey," Aunt Astrid said, her earlier scrutiny now completely gone.

"So what are we doing?" I asked, trying to sound enthusiastic but feeling that dusk settle over me again.

"Well, we are all getting massages first and then pedicures." Bea looked as if she had aged backward and was at least five years younger. This place must have been feeding her aura with good, holistic vibes. Too bad I couldn't say the same for myself.

"Well, that sounds fine," I lied. I didn't any more want a massage than I wanted a root canal, but they had gone through the trouble. This was to help me, they'd said. Okay, I'd play along.

I decided not to tell them about Officer Warner. What would be the point? He wouldn't be making any special appearances. I figured he was just a flirt, one of those guys who acted nice to *all* the girls. He probably thought I needed to be cheered up, and a quick conversation with Officer Devastatingly Handsome was just the ticket. I hate to admit it, but it hadn't hurt.

The Paranormal Lifestyle

I was sitting in a plush chair wearing nothing but underpants underneath the softest terrycloth robe on the planet when Olga came for me. Yes, her name really was Olga. She was a professional masseuse and was built like a linebacker for the Chicago Bears.

"You're with me, honey." Her soft voice was not at all in sync with her physical appearance of curly blond hair pulled back into a ponytail, a ruddy complexion, and thick, hardworking hands. I would have expected to see her on a farm or perhaps at a roadside construction site holding the STOP/ SLOW sign for cars to go by, but not at all in the white T-shirt and slacks that were typical masseuse attire.

I nodded.

"Now don't you worry. I'll take good care of you.

When we're done, you'll feel like a brand-new person." I looked up a good six inches to meet her eyes. They were a deep brown, and when she smiled, her cheeks pushing them into crescents, they reminded me of chocolate chip cookies with a bite taken out of them.

The thought of being a brand-new person was appealing. A new person who didn't talk to animals, who didn't know binding spells, and who had no clue about those things that lurk under beds and in shadows.

I scratched my head, trying to get the negative thoughts out of there.

Olga led me down a short hallway and opened the door to reveal a room I hadn't expected. When Bea had mentioned a massage and pedicure, I'd envisioned the massage would take place in a dimly lit room with scented candles, maybe a desktop water fountain, some New Age music floating through the air. I did hear soothing music, but this looked more like an examination room.

The walls were a pale blue. A small desk held a few nondescript oils in plain, medicinal-looking jars, and an iPod with tiny speakers provided the tunes. In the middle was the massage table.

"Okay, I find that most of my guests like to start

on their stomachs. It helps if you're not used to massages, and from the worry wrinkles in your brow, I can tell you might be a little apprehensive." She laid one of her giant paws against my arm, but it was soft and quite reassuring.

"I'll do that," I said.

"That's fine. Climb on up. I'm just going to turn my back to give you a moment's privacy, and then we can begin."

I nodded, hung my robe on the nearby hook, climbed up onto the table, and lay down on my stomach. Before I knew it, Olga had a crisp white sheet draped over me and was expertly rubbing the backs of my legs. I hadn't even known they were tired.

"So, how long have you been doing this?" I inquired, hoping that speaking during the session wasn't prohibited or discouraged. For the first time in a while, I wanted to talk.

"I've been a masseuse for over twenty years," she said quietly.

"How long have you worked here?"

"Let's see. Going on about seven years now. Yeah. Seven years."

My muscles tingled with joy. Olga worked on my legs and arms and started on my back.

"So what do you say about the stories of ghosts in your spa?"

I felt a slight hesitation in her hands, but then she continued kneading and twisting my muscles.

"Well, what the owners have reported is on the website," she said calmly.

I thought she was holding back, so I prodded a little further. "Have you ever experienced anything?"

"I'm not sure I'm supposed to repeat anything I've seen or heard," she said.

"I heard the clerk at the front desk talking about it. She told me people had seen a few things but that she couldn't say for sure because she hadn't seen anything."

"That sounds like Mia. Was she serious? Hair pulled back?"

"Yes."

"Yeah, well, she wouldn't tell anyone anything. That is the owner's niece. She's nice. Professional. But the fact that she's been here since she could walk yet says she's never seen *anything* is a pretty big stretch. Inhale and exhale slowly."

I did as I was told, letting my thoughts just sort of linger. What was I doing probing into all this? In two more nights, we were leaving, and who knew when we'd be back, if ever? What did I care if goblins or ghosties roamed this place? I was tired of the paranormal lifestyle, wasn't I? Hadn't it caused me more grief than anything else, even Darla Castellan? And what good was any of it if I couldn't use it for myself? Why couldn't I use it to get some winning lottery tickets or be able to cook better than Bea or right a few wrongs, level a few playing fields, or punish someone who had done me wrong?

"Boy, you must have a lot on your mind," Olga said. "It feels like I barely touched you, your muscles are so tight. Inhale again and exhale. There we are."

"So what did you see?" Maybe Olga's story would distract me from my own scary thoughts.

"If I tell you and you repeat it, I'll deny I ever said it. Just so we're clear." She began to rub my shoulders. "But I had one experience that I won't soon forget."

I heard Olga take a deep breath and begin her story.

When she'd first started working at the spa, she worked from six in the evening until midnight. She didn't have many clients, but she would get a few who were late check-ins or preferred evening hours.

"That way, management figured in case I caused anyone severe nerve damage or turned out to be a less-than-qualified masseuse, I wouldn't interfere with the busy hours. I didn't mind getting my feet wet that way working with the night owls. The night owls, that was what I called them."

On this particular evening, she had just finished with a young man who had been suffering from a migraine. He had come in at ten fifteen p.m. By eleven o'clock, he was feeling better and heading back to his room, but not before stopping at the Ambrosia Café for an iced green tea.

"It was beautiful warm weather outside. And one thing that I can't get over in this place is the scenery. At night there are lights throughout the grounds for anyone who wants to take a walk so they don't get lost or turned around. Most evenings until well past midnight, you can hear the voices of the late-night adventurers echo out along the trails. Boy, you've got one heck of a knot here."

I felt Olga dig into the middle of my back with her fist. I tried to relax, hoping she'd continue with her story.

"So, I went outside just for a little fresh air and to kill some time before I punched out. I walked out back, past the hot springs and just to the edge where the natural border of trees starts. There are beautiful solar lights scattered all around in addition to the electrically powered lights along the path, and…"

She let out a chuckle. "I saw a woman running like the devil was chasing her. She was wearing a dress that looked like it was dirty, maybe torn up a little. She was barefoot and ran past the hot springs to the back entrance that should have been locked already. Okay, I think I'm getting this now. Take a deep breath and let it out."

I did as I was told and felt the pressure from her thick hands as she rolled my muscles under her fingers.

"Well. The woman didn't come around the building, so I went to check if she had gotten inside, if a door was left unlocked. I thought maybe she was hurt or needed help. The back patio was empty."

"Do you think she might have gone around the other side of the patio opposite where you were standing?"

"You might think that, but the patio has an absolutely stunning decorative fence with ceramic tiles that would prevent anyone from going around. Especially from where this woman was."

I didn't say anything.

"I'd be willing to chalk that up to a trick of the eye, the lights playing tricks on me. Fatigue can make you think you see things you didn't. That wasn't what scared me. What scared me was the laughing."

"Laughing?"

"Have you ever heard a person who lives on the streets laugh?" she asked, her hands moving slowly and rhythmically. "It's an unsettling sound that makes you think they see something you're missing. It sounds hollow, you know."

I gripped the donut rest that my face was stuck in.

"Well, naturally I was worried that the woman had maybe been attacked or bitten by a snake or who knows. So, despite every fiber of my being telling me to just run away, I walked around the building." She stopped rubbing.

I turned over a little and leaned on my elbow, pulling the sheet modestly around me. Olga's friendly smile was still there, but I could see a shadow behind her eyes.

"I saw a girl there. Young woman, I should say, by the mosaic wall, crouched down. I cleared my throat, not wanting to scare her. But before I could say anything, the laughing started, and I froze. It wasn't a girl laughing. I couldn't even say it was a man laughing, but something thought me being glued to the sidewalk with sticky terror was pretty humorous.

I don't know how long I stood there. But when I finally felt in control enough to take a step, the woman snapped her head up, smiled at me and...as God is my witness...she climbed right up that wall like a spider."

Red

What?" I said, breathless. The image of the daddy longlegs with the human head came instantly to mind.

"She did, and when she got to the top, she just vanished or melted into the tile like a chameleon or something." Now it was time for Olga's laugh to be unsettling. "Why don't you roll onto your back and we'll get the rest of you fixed up."

I wanted to tell her what I had seen, but something wouldn't let me. If I was going to separate myself from this nonsense, there was no better time than the present.

"I don't believe that," I said, my words sounding harsher than I meant them to. "I mean, disappear? That is impossible."

"Sure it is. It's downright crazy. Loco. But it's what I saw."

"Well, our brains can convince us of almost anything. Voodoo priests in Haiti can kill people without ever laying a hand on them just by putting the idea in their victim's head."

"I've never been to Haiti." Olga chuckled.

"I'm sorry. It's just a wild story is all."

"Yeah." Olga seemed to be sorry she'd told me, and I should have been sorry for the way I was acting, but my insides felt like they were being torn in two directions. One part wanted to know more and see if there was something to all this. Another part wanted to laugh in Olga's face and tell her she was crazy.

We were quiet for a while, and then Olga spoke as if thinking out loud, like I wasn't even there.

"You know, the Wyandot Indians were at one time very prevalent in this area. Like all American Indians, they believed in shape-shifters, skin-walkers. Part of me thinks that has something to do with what I saw."

I couldn't really argue Native American folklore. What she was saying was true. But I had heard of humans changing into wolves or eagles or crows. Not some gross spider-human hybrid.

"Well, who knows?" Olga finally said. "Will you be enjoying the springs on your stay? I'd highly recommend it, especially for you. I've been working here, and you seem to be just as tense if not more so than when you stepped in. Are you doing okay?"

"Actually, it feels wonderful. You're doing fine." The massage did feel good, but I had to agree with her that I wasn't relaxed. I was far from being relaxed. I felt like I was teetering on the edge of something.

After the massage, I wrapped back up in my robe and went out into the waiting area, where my aunt and cousin were already sitting, sipping ice water and eating orange slices, rolling their heads and arching their backs with relief. I was ready for the performance of a lifetime.

"There you are. How do you feel?" Bea asked, scooting over so I could sit down next to her.

"I feel a lot better. I needed that." I was like a crinkled piece of cellophane that someone had crumpled up tightly, but it slowly snapped and twisted back into its original form, except now it had new crinkles in it. But when I looked into Bea's eyes, all I could see was that hopefulness, like she was waiting for the green light to not walk on eggshells anymore. "What's next?"

"Pedicures. Then I was thinking a walk along the grounds."

"I'd love a nice long walk," Aunt Astrid said, nodding.

"Then a late lunch. Is that okay with you?" Bea said, taking my hand and squeezing it.

"I'll be starving by then. Yes, sounds good." I managed a smile, blinking and hoping she wasn't picking up on anything when she held my hand.

"Great!" She squealed like a schoolgirl.

I sat through the pedicure just smiling and nodding as my aunt told stories about when she and Bea's father, my uncle, had been dating. How she had gone ice skating with him because he suggested it, unaware he was a hockey player while she could barely stand up straight.

"It wasn't all bad. It was the only way he could keep his arms around me without looking like a masher." And now she giggled like a schoolgirl.

My thoughts were dark. I couldn't help it. I used to love hearing about my family. I loved the lifestyles and histories and even the scandals, of which, because we had so many witches, we had an ample supply. But today, right now, I thought I was going to scream. My bones and muscles felt like they wanted to tear out of my skin and run. I just wanted to be alone.

"Hey, Cath. Remember that time you and Min and I were going to lunch and he mentioned that comic strip he saw about Al Capone?" Bea said, starting to laugh.

"Oh, yeah. It was like a hush had fallen over the restaurant just as he said Al Capone wasn't a bad guy. He was just misunderstood," I said, forcing a smile that made my cheeks ache. What was wrong with me?

I managed to get through the pedicure. When we went for the walk along the grounds, it was much easier to be quiet and not be noticed. I looked around at all the pretty plants whose foliage gave its most brilliant efforts in the fall. Bright-red bushes seemed to pop right out of the scenery.

I looked at the little plaque stuck in the ground in front of one that read Fire Bush. Then it gave some hard-to-read scientific name I didn't even try to repeat. But I didn't think I'd ever seen such a beautiful plant in my life. It stood out proudly against the grays and browns of the season as if to say, "Here I am! I made it! I'll only be here for a little while, but look at me! I'm gorgeous!"

I wished that I could just shrink down and hide

among those tall red stalks or maybe just be a rock snuggled in the dirt close by. I wanted to exist but to be something else. Something without cares. Something without family constantly asking if I was all right when it was obvious I wasn't, something that didn't feel loneliness or helplessness like I was feeling.

We made our way back to the spa, and I saw the mosaic tile wall Olga had talked about. It was beautiful. It was really big, too. No way could a person climb it.

But she didn't say it was a person. She said it was a person that turned into some kind of spider. Like the one you saw on the tree. A shape-shifter.

I shook my head. I didn't want to hear that voice. The one I had been listening to for all these years. It accepted that unseen world of demons and angels and dimensions where Bigfoot and the chupacabra lived. The overwhelming urge to run settled into my bones, but I couldn't make a move while my aunt and Bea walked next to me. Thankfully their chatter had died down.

Just lunch, Cath. Just lunch and then you can get to your room, lock the door, and try and rest. I tried to tell myself that was all I needed, but I knew it wasn't true. If I slept for ten days, it wouldn't change the fact that I didn't want to be *me* anymore. I didn't want to be anyone.

Swallowing hard, I bit my tongue until the feeling of blubbering like a baby passed.

Lunch came with beautifully arranged plates of healthy green stuff as the feng shui of the room and strategically hung crystals optimized the good mojo and flow of energy.

With monumental effort, I managed to contribute to the conversation. I tossed in a crack here and there, gave an opinion now and again, and mostly tried to just shovel the food into my mouth so the talk could weave around me instead of pulling me into it. By the time we stood up to go, the sun was starting to set.

"Your toes look so pretty," Aunt Astrid said, slipping her arm through mine as we walked to the elevator while Bea chit-chatted with the hostess for a moment. "You should wear red more often."

I shook my head. I'd only picked red because I didn't want to stand around for hours trying to make a meaningless decision on the color of my toenails. I certainly didn't want to draw attention to myself like those bright-red bushes out there on the grounds.

Before I could get too deep in thought, I felt as if

I was being watched. I looked up and caught Aunt Astrid studying me.

"There's something there," she mumbled more to herself than to me. "Something..." Her eyes floated around me as if I was giving off vapors.

"What are you talking about?" I barked, causing Bea, the hostess, a couple of patrons, and Aunt Astrid to look at me in surprise. I cleared my throat.

Aunt Astrid's gaze became focused and serious.

"There's no need to take that tone with me, Cath. I was just thinking out loud."

Tell her, that inner voice hissed. *Tell her you hate being here and you're tired of the whole witch thing! Tell her you want your own life!*

"I...I didn't mean anything. I guess I am really more tired than I thought. Maybe I'm coming down with something." I rubbed my forehead and averted my eyes from my aunt's, looking down at the floor, down the hallway, and up at the ceiling.

"It's all right, honey," she said.

"What's going on?" Bea asked, looking concerned and serious. Those two were like a tag team. I'd never have a chance with those two against my one.

"I'm sorry. I just belted out louder than I expected, that's all. My bad." I patted my aunt on the shoulder and quickly walked to the elevator bank, pressing the UP button and praying the wait wouldn't be long.

No one spoke. We just stood there awkwardly. Finally the ping of the elevator and the sliding doors broke it up.

"Maybe we should skip dinner tonight," Bea said sadly.

"I'm stuffed. I can't even think of eating another bite," Aunt Astrid added.

Inside, a wave of relief washed over me, but I didn't say a word. Before the doors had even slid completely open, I had squeezed through and was heading toward my room, pulling the little plastic key from my pocket. I was almost running and didn't dare look back to see my aunt and cousin talking, conspiring, and gossiping about me. I didn't need it. I just wanted to be alone. To rest.

Once the door slid shut, I let out a deep sigh. I walked to the window, opened the sliding door, and stepped out onto the balcony. The sky looked beautiful, with a thin layer of intense orange then pink blending into indigo before the blackness of night consumed it all. I looked down at my toes. The bright red color stood out against my pale skin like blood. That was when I heard a fluttering sound.

At first I thought a piece of paper had blown in

the slight breeze, but when I turned, I saw the little bird on the ground. It must have flown into the glass, because it was lying there barely moving.

"Hey. Hey, little fellow. Are you okay?" I asked in my head.

"I don't want it to come," the little guy replied.

"What? Don't want what to come? I think you hurt your head. Just stay still. You'll be all right."

No response. It fluttered and twitched, but it was not going to make it. The thought of picking it up and bringing it to Bea crossed my mind, but before I could make a move, the little beast stopped breathing. Its onyx eyes shone in death. It had brown wings with a little bit of yellow and a white belly. Some kind of finch if I had to guess.

I stood there looking at the little creature. First I'd had to see those cannibal chipmunks and now this. The deer killed all along the drive up here? What the hell was happening? And why was I scared of feeling like I had no feelings?

Exhaustion swept over me. I left the little body on the balcony, closed the door, and locked it. Then I pulled the curtains shut.

The bed was the only place I wanted to be. I didn't even bother getting undressed. I just kicked off my flip-flops and lay down. Within seconds I was asleep. But it wasn't a restful sleep. It was a never-ending swirling of darkness, and I kept thinking the door was open. I was sleeping with the door wide open, and things were coming down the hallway. I could hear dragging noises, like someone had a bad leg that was wrapped in a bag of wet, sloshy noodles.

The door is open! I heard my own thoughts cry out in a panic. But I was so tired. My eyes couldn't be pried open except for a few seconds at a time.

Anyone could walk in if I left the door open. Anyone at all could just come in and shut the door behind them, and then I'd be trapped.

Carcass

No, Cath. It's just a dream. Open your eyes and you'll see the door's closed. It's closed and you're already trapped.

My eyes popped open and darted around the dark room. I tried to move and felt the sharp pain in my neck and back. What was going on? Was something holding me down, pulling at my neck and shoulders? Where? What? I flailed my arms, all the while squeezing my eyes tight from the pain. Nothing. I didn't make contact with anything. Freezing in mid-swing, I strained my eyes through the dark of the room. I was alone.

The door was closed. The orange glow from the switch in the bathroom was the only light I could see clearly. I tried to sit up but couldn't. Something was pulling my spine, twisting, bending it like a pipe snake.

Gritting my teeth, I slowly rolled onto my stomach. The pressure wasn't as bad on my stomach. Reaching for the phone, I dialed Bea's room. Within seconds, she and Aunt Astrid were knocking urgently on my door.

"Okay!" I shouted with tears running down my cheeks. "I'm okay! I'm coming!" I rolled out of the bed and dragged myself along the floor. The idea of standing up straight made me tremble. What had Olga done to me?

Pulling the door latch, I looked up to see Bea and Aunt Astrid looking down at me in horror.

"Get her inside. Quick, before someone sees us."

"I swear I'm going to sue that masseuse!" I cried. "What did she do to me?"

"It isn't the masseuse's fault, Cath. I was afraid of this," Bea shut the door, locking the deadbolt and setting the security bar in place. She joined me on the bed.

I was still on my stomach, and I felt her hands squeezing my legs. Her hands were warm and comforting, but her words were anything but.

"Here's one. Another one."

"What about here?" Aunt Astrid asked.

"Maybe? Yes, another one. I think the main problem is here," Bea said as if I wasn't there.

I was starting to get angry. "What are you two talking about?" I sobbed. The pain was terrible. "You both need to shut up and help me…"

"Cath. I need you to lie perfectly still. Don't move. Don't flinch. And whatever you do, don't scream." Bea's voice rumbled like the thunder that foretells rain coming beneath dark, low-lying clouds.

"Don't scream?"

She quickly grabbed a pillow. I thought she was going to kneel down on it, but she just placed it in front of her. Crossing her legs, she sat in front of me and took my arms, pulling them painfully up alongside my ears.

"Bea, I don't want any magic! I don't want any at all! I'm so scared of all this and sick of it ruining my life."

"That's fine, Cath. After this, we don't ever have to use magic again, but right now…"

"I'm serious! I don't want this anymore. Stop! Stop pulling at me! You're hurting me!" I was crying outright. I still felt the love for my family. I could feel my voice rising. Soon it would be so loud people would come running. And then my aunt and Bea would be in trouble. Why weren't they listening to me? I struggled to get up but felt the heavy weight of my aunt plop down on the backs of my legs.

"This is where it is," Bea said in a low voice, not to me, of course, but to her mother. Rubbing her hands together, she began to mutter some words I didn't immediately recognize.

"Please, Bea. Please, no magic. Let me up. I'm feeling better. Honest I am. I just want to be normal. I just want this pain to go away."

Bea held both my hands in one of hers, and I was shocked to feel the viselike grip she had on me. Jake must have taught her that just in case she ever had to subdue a suspect or something. Her knuckles were white and strained, but she wasn't letting go. With her other hand, she gently stroked my head.

"You just hush now, honey. Don't you worry about a thing. We've got it now," she soothed.

I managed to get up just a little to my elbows. I looked up at Bea, who was looking down at me like I was a pool of those little plastic ducks and she was sizing up which one would yield the best prize.

"Just let me up, Bea. I'm okay now," I pleaded. I watched Bea's eyes, and they seemed to focus on the space just above my head.

"Your meal ticket is over," she hissed.

Why was she telling me this? I had never thought

of her and Aunt Astrid that way. Was this what they really felt about me?

"You've been a drain. You've been hurting her. Time for you to get a taste of your own medicine. *Habathaaa...*" Bea said this last word, which I had never heard before, with such hatred in her voice that I began to shake.

I tried to pull away, but she wouldn't let me go. Aunt Astrid leaned so much farther onto me that she was pushing my hips and stomach into the hard bed. I was starting to have trouble breathing.

"Let go!" Bea said and pulled my arms taut. It felt like my head was being pulled from my shoulders. Bea said more words I didn't understand. Witchy words and old chants from something that Aunt Astrid had obviously shared with her and not with me.

"I said you let her go." Bea's forehead was covered with sweat. She quickly dropped my hands, and before I could squirm or swat her away, she had one knee on them and had her hands on my shoulders. Her grip tore into my shoulders.

My breath froze in my throat. My face was contorted in pain that shot through my spine and could only come out my eyes in tiny teardrops.

"Show yourself, you coward," Aunt Astrid

chimed in this time. She pushed down on the small of my back until I was afraid I was going to suffocate from lack of oxygen.

And just then the image of those cannibalistic chipmunks bounced into my head.

"Oh, no!" My words were barely audible. "I'm the carcass! You're fighting over my bones! This is some sick ritual I wasn't aware of, isn't it?" It was like those dreams when you are trying to scream. You're using everything inside you, all your strength and energy, but all that comes out is a whisper too quiet to even be heard in church.

"Breathe, Catherine! Take one deep breath then look in the mirror!"

A floor-to-ceiling mirror stood next to the writing desk. We were right in front of it.

"Take a deep breath and look, now!" Bea ordered.

I did as I was told and turned my head.

"Look, Cath! That's what's been hurting you! That piece-of-garbage bottom feeder!"

For a brief second, I saw a shadow, a glint of something around my head and shoulders.

"There's nothing there," I whimpered. "You're trying to kill me."

"Look at them, Cath. And help us get rid of them

once and for all." Bea's weight on my hands was making them tingle.

I shut my eyes tight, feeling the hot rain of tears spill over. When I opened my eyes and looked in the mirror again, I gasped in horror.

A Feast of a Lifetime

✦

It was on my back, its eight legs digging into me—but not into my skin. It was digging into my soul as it flickered and blinked in and out of view. My eyes widened, and I wanted to scream as I saw not just the two huge, round eyes staring at me but the four little ones underneath them as well. Its fangs were buried deep in my shoulder blades.

It was the size of a healthy teenager. That was bad enough. But I saw smaller ones, too, the size of rats. They ran up and down my body as if I were some jungle floor they were used to scurrying around on.

Bea began to chant while I began to hyperventilate. I had never seen or heard of anything like this before. My breath wasn't filling my lungs. My face was turning beet red. Aunt Astrid leaned and reached over me, pulling the pillow into my face. I thought for sure she was trying to smother me until Bea gave a loud command, and the searing pain in my legs stopped. I looked in the mirror again even though I didn't want to.

It glowered at me. It wasn't exactly like the thing I had seen on the tree, but it was similar. The two big eyes were bottomless. Its fangs hung down like the jowls of an ogre, and it sneered, pushing itself farther into my shoulders. I screamed into the pillow, thankful that my aunt had put it there. Had she not, there would have been police breaking down the door by now for sure.

"Let her go!" Bea let go of my shoulders, rubbed her hands together quickly, and placed them on my shoulder blades, where the fangs looked to be pulsing and throbbing inside my aura. "You Habatha can feed no more. Go! Leave her and starve!"

It was almost instantaneous. After Bea said those words, I felt a flash of blinding pain. I wasn't sure what happened after that, if I was out for a few seconds, minutes, or hours, but when I opened my eyes, I felt as if I had been asleep for days.

I pulled my head out of the pillow and saw it was drenched in sweat. Carefully, I pulled my arms in and put my hands underneath me to push myself up.

I felt no pain of any kind. I looked up and saw Bea, sitting on the floor next to the mirror, covered in sweat, too, and breathing hard.

Quickly I rolled over to see Aunt Astrid leaning against the closed sliding door to the balcony, also disheveled and worn out like a used and discarded bathroom towel.

I tried to speak. I wanted to know what had happened. But as I saw my aunt there, the only woman I had ever known to take care of me, to love me, to protect me after my mother had gone, I was overcome with shame. All those horrible thoughts, those cruel remarks and hateful feelings, came crashing back to me as if a wall had been smashed to pieces by a big steel ball to let them all through.

"I didn't mean it," I begged. "I didn't mean any of it." She opened her arms wide to me. Quickly, I crawled over to her and fell into them as I had done many times as a child. Burying my face in her neck, I cried and cried until I didn't think I had any liquid left in my body.

"It's okay, honey. It's all right. You don't need to apologize. We knew something was wrong with you. We just didn't know what."

"We still think there is something wrong with you," Bea said, her voice giving away the smile on her face. "But it's a thing even magic can't fix, so, well, we're just used to it is all."

I turned around and finally got a grip on myself.

"I have been horrible to you guys. I am so sorry. I didn't mean any of that stuff I said. I was just feeling so..."

"We know, honey."

I took a deep breath.

"Bea, what in the world was that thing? Those things?"

Bea cracked her knuckles and pushed herself off the floor.

"Astral spiders."

"What?" I felt my body convulse involuntarily, as the idea of any kind of spiders gave me serious heebie-jeebies. "What the hell is an astral spider?"

"They are pretty rare, but they are parasites, plain and simple. They break into this dimension, look for a person with low energy, latch on, and, well, do what spiders do," Bea said matter-of-factly while walking over and plopping down on the bed.

"And that is?" I wasn't sure I really wanted to know, but I had a pretty good idea what Bea was going to say.

"They suck your energy out little bit by little bit. You know how so many people today claim to have depression. No, they don't. They have astral spiders sucking the life right out of them." Bea yawned as if the conversation was about watching paint dry.

"You saw it first, didn't you?" I looked at Aunt Astrid.

She smoothed my hair away from my eyes and rubbed my cheek gently. "I had a feeling something was there," she said, narrowing her eyes. "It was hiding pretty well. You hadn't been yourself, and we both knew something was wrong. We just hoped it was something we'd be able to deal with."

Bea added, "That massage was just the thing to get your energy flowing. The spider was gorging itself and got very careless. It obviously thought it could fight us off through you, but little did it know we rarely listen to what you want anyways. We would have gone against your wishes as easily as if we were changing our shirts."

I chuckled.

"Where did I get this thing?"

"Toilet seat," Aunt Astrid said.

I whipped my head around to see her smirk spread into a smile until she burst out laughing.

"I'll give you one guess as to where you picked up that creepy crawler."

My body slumped.

"Don't tell me it was the Prestwick house," I said, feeling exhausted just saying the name of that place.

"That's what I think. That place changed all of us a little. But you seemed to suffer the real brunt of it," Bea said. I saw her eyes flick to my aunt's face then back to me again.

"Why do you think that is?" I said humbly. I clenched my teeth, bracing myself for what I was going to hear. I was the weak link in the group. My powers were limited, and I was stubborn and could sometimes be rude, and I thought of myself almost all the time. Sheesh, what did anyone see in me anyways? My family? My friends? I was a big mess and caused more trouble than I was worth.

"If I had to guess, it is because you are a good person. I'm old. An astral spider isn't going to waste its time on someone like me. Bea has the gift of healing, so she'd spot the thing right away if it latched onto her. You? You are so alive. Full of piss and vinegar, as my old grandma used to say. It saw the feast of a lifetime with you."

"So it isn't because I'm weak? Because I ruined the spell on the house and now we have to go back every once in a while for paranormal upkeep?"

"No, honey. It has nothing at all to do with what

you *did* at the house. It has to do with the fact you were *at* the house. That's all." My aunt patted my back.

I pushed myself up and turned, offering both hands to my aunt to help her to her feet as well. Sniffling back a few tears, I nodded.

"So, now that that thing is off you, how do you feel?"

I rolled my head, shrugged, stood on my toes, and stretched my arms over my head.

"Feeling good. I guess I won't be suing Olga after all." But my eyes widened with worry as I was hit with a memory. "But I saw something like that, that astral spider outside on a tree. I swear it was the same kind of thing."

"Oh, I believe it was," Bea said, standing up from the bed. "I saw a few along our walk. This is obviously a feeding ground for them, since people are opening up and letting the positive energies flow all willy-nilly. They won't be bothering you anymore, Cath. I can promise you that." Bea looked very sure, but I couldn't say I was totally convinced.

"That house!" I said, stomping my foot. "That house hurt me...really bad." I stood straight and looked my family in the eyes. "Everything fell apart in there. I messed up going after Blake, then you all had to come rescue me like a rookie, and you guys couldn't get prepared, and I can't shake the feeling that something, something bad, has planted a seed, you know?" I said, rubbing a spot in the middle of my chest. "And I'm terrified it's going to take root and grow into something...horrible."

"It got to all of us, Cath. There was just something about you, like Mom said, that it wanted. It tore you up, left an open wound, and that spider found it."

I shivered again.

"We also know that the whole Blake and Darla thing has been eating away at you."

I bit my lower lip and shrugged.

"You save a guy's life, and this is the thanks you get," I mumbled, making circles in the carpet with my foot. "I guess he's just more into the high-maintenance, damsel-in-distress type."

My family said nothing, but I knew what they were thinking. *Poor Cath.*

"I'm hungry. Anybody want to go downstairs and grab a late-night snack? Those greens for lunch just didn't do the job."

"Told you," Bea said to Aunt Astrid. "I knew when she didn't finish that salad that something was wrong with her. Eating like a bird, that is not my cousin."

"So is that a yes? You guys coming with?"

"I'm beat. I'm going to go to bed," my aunt said, scratching the back of her head and heading toward the door.

"Sorry, cuz, you wore me out," Bea added. "But tomorrow we have facials, mud baths, and hot springs." She leaned in and gave me a kiss on the cheek.

"That sounds awesome," I said, because it really did.

We said our good nights, but I was full of energy. I hadn't felt this good in weeks. I welcomed the anger I felt toward that Prestwick house and swore if it were the last thing I did, someday, somehow I'd burn the whole thing to the ground. But right now wasn't the time. I had more important issues to address.

I went down to the dining room. Waving over the waitress, I pointed to the late-night menu.

"Don't you guys have any meat burgers?"

Good Old-Fashioned Murder

A fter a pretty satisfying black bean burger with sweet potato fries and a Green-Eyed Monster smoothie packed with kale, spinach, apple, banana, and pineapple, I returned to my room, hopped onto the bed, and snapped on the television.

Thankfully, I found one of my favorite guilty pleasures on: a really horribly acted crime show about detectives in New York who always picked the wrong guy as the culprit, interrogated him, told his wife, the papers, and anyone else who would listen, only to have to go back and say oops. Every episode they did this, and yet they still had their badges. How would that work in real life?

Happily, I pondered these thoughts, made really

snide comments to the characters, and ordered an onion blossom from the all-night menu. I ate in bed and finally fell asleep...only to wake up two hours later in the middle of the night to the fire alarm going off.

⚜

"AUNT ASTRID, ANY IDEA WHAT THIS IS ALL about?" I asked as I walked up to her and Bea in the parking lot. The spa staff had herded us all out there. Thankfully, it was cool but not cold, and the stretchy pajamas Bea had picked out for me were enough to keep out the chill. Both Bea and Astrid had managed to snag their robes before slipping out. I felt a little naked beside them.

"It's not a fire, that's for sure," she said.

"Your psychic radar tell you that?" I asked.

"No. I don't smell any smoke, though. Do you?"

I sniffed the air and shook my head, smiling.

"Me neither," said Bea as she looked around. Three fire trucks came rumbling up the hill along with two squad cars and two ambulances. It looked like the Macy's Thanksgiving Day parade. Everyone moved back to give the first responders room to do their thing.

All the red and blue flashing lights turned the spa into a bizarre outdoor discotheque without the music. Trying to watch what was going on was like watching an anthill. There was too much movement for me to focus on any one spot for too long.

"They're dead," Aunt Astrid said in a whisper. "Sisters. They died in their room."

"Of what?" Bea asked.

"I don't know. Not yet."

"Please let this be a good old-fashioned murder," I mumbled. Bea and Aunt Astrid looked at me with hands on their hips.

"What? I'm not trying to be mean. I just would really like to enjoy those facials and mud baths tomorrow instead of searching out some interdimensional troublemaker. Is that so wrong?"

Bea raised her eyebrows and shrugged as she looked at her mother.

"I just don't know about you two," Aunt Astrid said, shaking her head. "Glad you're feeling better, Cath."

"Hey, if this is something paranormal, I wonder if..." I choked on the words. "Oh, no." I swallowed hard, took Bea by the hand, and pulled her in front of me.

"What is wrong with you?" she scolded.

"Nothing. Just stand where you are."

"I'm trying to see…"

"Don't move!" I stage whispered.

"Hey!" came a familiar male voice. "Hey, Cath!"

I stepped out from behind Bea, pulling my hair off my face nervously and smiling.

"Hi, Officer." Suddenly I remembered. "Oh, gosh! Is your sister okay? Her guests?"

"Yeah. I called her on her cell when the emergency call came over the dispatch." He smiled, that dimple winking at me in the dim light. He was so handsome in his uniform. I shook my head to focus.

"I'm sorry. This is my aunt, Astrid Greenstone, and my cousin, Bea Williams. This is Officer Tom Warner."

Officer Warner shook their hands politely. I did everything I could to avoid the surprised and all-too-interested looks of my fellow witches.

"I'm glad your sister is okay. Lucky you were close by, right? In case they needed you." I had no idea what I was saying. My hands were sweating, so I kept rubbing them together. Taking two steps away from Astrid and Bea, I managed to get Officer Warner out of their earshot.

"I wasn't here to check on her," he said, slipping

his fingers into the loops on his utility belt. "You didn't give me a phone number, so I had no way of calling to check on you."

"Me?" I laughed out loud. "Oh, trust me. I'm okay. Yes, sir. I'm fine. Right as rain."

"You got your toes painted," he said, pulling out his flashlight and shining it on them for a brief second. "Red. That's my favorite color."

Thankful for the dark of night, I was pretty sure Officer Warner couldn't see me blush. I wrapped one foot around the other ankle and couldn't think of a single thing to say. Instead I grinned like a lunatic, I'm sure.

"Well," he said, still smiling. "Now that I see you are okay and your toes are colored, I think I can get going. But there is one problem."

"If it's about that picture of me in the post office, I can explain."

"Funny," he said, looking me in the eyes. His were kind, and I got the feeling he would have liked to stay and chat longer, but duty was calling. "No, see, I had to make the trip all the way up here to check on you. You kind of owe me."

"What?"

"Yeah. You know, there could be a bank being

robbed right now, and I'm all the way up here checking on you. So I think that deserves dinner or something."

"Or something?" I huffed. "I didn't tell you to come all the way up here. That was your choice. I can take care of myself."

"Really? What makes you so tough?"

My heart skipped a beat when he asked me that question. Normally, I'd just shy away from it. I'd shrug or shake my head and not give an answer, but not this time. Without flinching, I spoke.

"I'm kind of a ghost hunter. I don't scare easily." It wasn't the total truth, but it wasn't exactly a lie, either. I wasn't going to let what had happened with Blake happen again. So if this guy turned tail and ran, which he probably would, then I'd be no worse off than I had been when I first got here. *He can think I'm weird all he wants. No skin off my nose. No ma'am. No sir.*

"No kidding?" His intense gaze made me feel proud. "I'd like to hear more about that."

"Really? What makes *you* so tough?"

"Let's just say I appreciate life's mysteries. I'll be seeing you soon, Cath Greenstone."

As he walked away, turning to give me one last

look before he disappeared into the crowd of EMTs, police, and firemen, I tried to look everywhere but at my relatives. Finally, after studying every shrub, leaf, car, and pebble on the ground, I looked at them and smiled.

"What?" My eyelids fluttered with innocent concern.

"Officer Warner is very cute and very interested in you," Bea said. "Would you like me to have Jake check him out?"

"He already knows Jake, and no, I don't want you to. If he's a weirdo, I'll find out on my own. Besides, don't we have bigger issues at hand?" I waved toward the two gurneys being wheeled out with both passengers completely covered with sheets. Passing in front of this solemn scene were two figures that were more than familiar.

"Jake is here," Bea said, pleasantly surprised.

"And Blake Samberg bringing up the rear," my aunt added, sounding like she was naming a slightly offensive ingredient in a bowl of soup. I loved her for that.

"Hey, honey," Jake said, stepping up to Bea and kissing her on the cheek. Blake had stopped to peek morbidly underneath the sheets of both victims.

"Glad to see you are all okay. We got the call about the victims, and since the Muskox is in the Wonder Falls jurisdiction, this is now our issue. Can't say I'm all that surprised."

"Do you have any details?" Aunt Astrid asked, looking all kinds of concerned.

Jake tilted his head to the right.

"Fool me once, Mom," Jake said, shaking his finger at her. I had no idea what he was talking about, but my aunt's face looked guilty.

"What? She fooled you, too? Now you know how I felt. Shameful is all I have to say." I folded my arms and looked down my nose at both Bea and Aunt Astrid.

"They sure did. Told me they were just going to this spa to help you feel better. Hot springs, mud masks, and all that girlie stuff. Turns out the place is not only famous for natural hot springs but for UFO sightings, ghostly apparitions, unexplained phenomena, missing persons, and a string of weird deaths over the past couple of decades that aren't directly tied to the place but are suspiciously connected."

"Bea, how could you?" I whined dramatically, placing my hand over my heart.

"I didn't know anything about the UFOs," Bea said.

"A little basic Internet research spilled the beans on this place. I'd like it if you guys would check out now. No one is going to try and make you pay for the rooms. I'll see to that."

"No, Jake," Bea said. "We had nothing to do with this. Our stay has been relatively uneventful and very relaxing until the management herded us out here like cattle. Why don't you let me take a look at the women, and I'll tell you—"

"Bea, you know I can't do that."

Sticking her lips out like a fish, Bea nodded.

"But before Samberg comes," Jake continued, "have you guys, you know, sensed anything?"

We all looked at each other as if we weren't sure what he was insinuating.

"No, honey," Bea said.

"Nothing strange going on while we've been here," Aunt Astrid added.

I shook my head as well.

Looking past Jake, I saw Blake tug the sheet back over the second body and start walking in our direction. Part of me just wanted to run and hide, and another part of me wanted to run up and slap him across the face. Since my duel was internal, I just ended up standing still and shifting awkwardly from one foot to another.

"Evening, ladies," he said in his normal quiet and condescending way.

"Detective," my aunt said, nodding in Blake's direction.

"What did you get?" Jake asked.

"Not much. The victims were sisters. This was their first time here. From the markings on their bodies and the blue lips, I'd say they suffered some kind of poisoning."

"What, like eating-too-much-seafood kind of poisoning or adding-antifreeze-to-your-smoothie poisoning?" I asked Jake, more interested in the facts than in who was presenting them.

"We won't know that until we run some blood tests," Blake said, but I didn't even see his mouth move.

I nodded and began to think. What could poison a person at this place? The spa didn't serve alcohol or meat. The chances of the staff using bleach or any harsh chemicals in the holistic, all-natural environment were probably nil.

"Do you have some thoughts?" Blake asked. He had been staring at me.

I didn't like that. It was too confusing. The guy went to great lengths back home to stay away from me, and now he wanted to pick my brain like he had when we sat in my car together outside the Roy house. That wasn't fair or nice. I shook my head. Any ideas or sparks or hunches I had I'd share with Bea and Aunt Astrid. Blake Samberg was on his own.

Jake said, "I'll need to take a look at the victims before they get transported to the morgue. We'll have to notify next of kin."

"They wore no wedding rings, but that doesn't necessarily mean anything," Blake added.

I wrapped my arms around myself and rubbed my skin briskly to chase away the chill that ran up my spine. It was a warmer night than usual, but I got the feeling something was standing back watching this whole thing take place. I wondered if the astral spiders were circling, looking for anyone with a weak spot, a tender area like Smaug from *The Hobbit* had on his belly that was big enough for only one single arrow to pierce.

"You probably should have worn your robe," Blake said to me, studying me like he always did as if I was some kind of strange bacterium he was observing. Normally I would have rolled my eyes or had some kind of smart quip about how observant he was or how high the bar was for detectives these days, but that fire had gone out. How could he even pretend to be interested in what I was or wasn't doing when he obviously had his hands more than full with Darla Castellan?

Instead I just looked away and walked a few steps away from everyone. I heard Jake tell Bea they were staying on the scene for some interviews and to investigate the room. The sun would probably be rising by the time they were done.

Looking up into the sky, I was amazed at how many stars I saw. It made me feel small. Had I seen this view with that horrible creature sucking on me, I was afraid I would have thrown myself off a cliff in despair, but not now. It was comforting to know so much was out there.

It was beautiful and deep, and I was even moved to wonder at the astral spiders that did exist alongside angels and devils and ghosts, with us people thrown into the mix. There wasn't really time to dwell on a broken heart, right? It was such a miniscule speck compared to those great spaces above and below the planet.

I heard the men walking off and returned to Bea and Aunt Astrid.

"It will be hard to get into the room with Jake and Blake there," Bea said, watching them speak to the spa manager, who had greeted them with an outstretched hand.

"But they said it sounded like poison," I said. "That sounds like someone with a vendetta or an ax to grind. Not a job for us witches. Maybe it was suicide? Whatever the case may be, I don't think it involves us. Do you?"

"They were in room 116. You mentioned the man who saw something in there," my aunt reminded me.

"Yeah, but he said he was terrified by something. Not that something tried to kill him or poison him. He just got spooked. The website obviously states this for its customers, so I'm not convinced this is a job for us to look into."

The spa staff began herding all of us back inside. It was then that I saw something out of the corner of my eye off to my right. I thought I saw a woman running like the devil was chasing her to the back of the spa. She was carrying her shoes. Her hair was long and wild. I held my breath for just a moment and listened. I couldn't tell if it was the wind or not, but I could have sworn I heard laughing. I looked in the direction the girl had run and listened again.

There it was, the laughing. Olga had been right. It was a sick, deranged sound that made me think of yellowed eyes and cheeks flushed with fever. However, the sound wasn't coming from the back of the building. It sounded like it was right beside me. When I turned slowly to look, I saw I was all alone.

My feet wanted to run, but I decided keeping my cool, even just the appearance of being cool, would be a better tactic. Something was out there in that beautiful landscape, and it had found a way in.

Pellucidium

The warmth of the spa lobby felt like a flannel shirt over my shoulders. The entire room was alive with people talking and speculating, and the staff behind the check-in counter was busy answering questions and dealing with quite a few upset guests. *The spa is going to suffer quite a few refunds and early checkouts,* I thought as I spied Bea talking quickly with Jake as Aunt Astrid made her way to the elevator.

"What is Bea talking to Jake about?" I asked when I caught up to her.

"I'm not sure. But I don't think he's happy," Aunt Astrid said. "If he saw what I was seeing right now, he wouldn't be happy at all."

"What are you seeing? Please don't tell me it's more astral spiders."

My aunt narrowed her eyes and looked around the entire lobby.

"No. But things are not what they seem around here. It isn't like this all the time. Those girls in the backs of those two ambulances were chosen for something."

"What, like sacrifices?"

Aunt Astrid nodded and looked at me.

"We need to get into that room."

Bea walked back to us.

"Well, that is going to be darn near impossible," Bea said in a hushed voice as she pretended to be straightening her robe. "Jake and the others are going to be here through the night. They need to question everyone. They'll be taking photos, dusting for prints, all the usual stuff. And he wants us to check out when he leaves tomorrow."

"But I feel better," I said, selfishly pouting. "I haven't soaked in the hot springs yet. This trip was to make *me* feel better, right? We don't even know if this is a case for us. Maybe it was a suicide pact. Perhaps it was just accidental, you know?"

"I need to get into that room," Aunt Astrid said. "And the sooner the better. The energy and trace elements might still be strong enough for me to get a reading or see a flashback or something."

Instead of standing around looking suspicious when the elevator dinged, we piled in. The doors slid shut, and Aunt Astrid told us her crazy plan to get into that room.

⊗

"WHAT DO YOU CALL IT?" I ASKED, scratching my head.

"Pellucidium. It's a trick to make myself sort of invisible. Well, not invisible. More like a chameleon. I'll blend in."

"Mom, if the last time you did this was over twenty years ago and it kept you in bed for about a week, why do you think it is a good idea to do it now?"

"That was before I got good at it and learned how to pace myself. Plus, I want to know what is in that room, don't you?"

"Well, yeah," Bea said. "But not at your expense."

"I'm just going to get one of the officers to open the balcony door. Then I'll just lie in wait until everyone leaves and let you guys in. Easy peasy."

"Easy peasy, she says." Bea looked at me, rolling her eyes. "So there's no talking you out of it?"

That was a dumb question, and Bea realized it right after the words tumbled out of her mouth.

"Okay, Mom. When are you going to make your move?"

"The easiest thing to do is wait. I'll just stand outside the door. Sooner or later, the boys will be done with their questioning."

"How are you going to just stand outside the door?" I asked.

"Like this." Aunt Astrid rubbed her hands together and raised them over her head, chanting what sounded like the Chinese practice words I always tried to pronounce from the backs of the fortunes inside fortune cookies. As she lowered her arms over her head, her face, her neck, and all the way down her body, she became like the elegant pearl-and-gold tapestry wallpaper that covered the interior of the elevator. If I looked hard, I could see her eyes blinking and a wide smile on her lips.

"You love this, don't you?" I asked.

"I do," she said, the wallpaper rippling around her lips. "I used to keep an eye on Bea this way when she was a little girl."

"Oh, Lord. Please don't tell me things like that," Bea said, sounding very much like me. I laughed.

"I hope you stopped once she and Jake started dating."

"You two are terrible," Bea said, averting her eyes to the numbers at the top of the door.

"I'll ride the elevator back downstairs. Once I'm in the room and alone, I'll call your rooms from inside. Come around back to the balcony, and I'll let you in."

Bea and I nodded and got off the elevator on the third floor. Two people, a man and a woman, their bags packed, were hustling onto the elevator.

"I just can't stay in a place where people died," the man said to the woman, who nervously nodded in agreement. Aunt Astrid would get to hear more of their conversation as they rode the elevator back down.

"Little do they know how many people die all over the place every day," I said. "I think the challenge would be finding a place where someone didn't die. Good luck with that."

"Right?" Bea said, pulling out her plastic key. "I'll see you in a little bit. Try and get some rest before Mom calls."

I nodded and headed down the hallway to my room. Once inside, I snapped on the television, piled the pillows high on top of each other, and got comfortable. Who knew how long this was going to take? Aunt Astrid could be down there matching the carpet and loveseat for a couple of hours before they finished going over the place. And maybe there was still a chance that the whole thing could be a normal cause of death. Suicide. Overdose. Maybe the death of those two women was something that didn't have a supernatural influence.

I tried to focus on possibilities, but my mind kept drifting back to Blake. His being here made me mad. He was half the reason I'd had to be shanghaied and brought here.

It would have been easy for me to blame Blake for everything. But a part of me still held out hope that maybe it was all a mistake. He had been nice to me in the car outside the Roy house. Well, he had been annoying and condescending, but it was in his usual way. I could deal with that. Plus, his mind worked in such a fascinating and calculated way that I was finding it hard to believe he could have anything in common with Darla.

I looked down at myself and thought Darla had quite a bit that I didn't. I could hate her for being mean to me, but I couldn't begrudge her the fact that she was blessed with so many things going for her. Looks. Money. What else did a girl need to get by?

Common sense and dry wit couldn't pay for a spin cycle at the Laundromat.

Oh, snap out of it, Cath! I shook my head and pulled my hair back. *You sound like a high school freshman.* It was true. I was starting to annoy myself, and that was quite an accomplishment, because usually I was more than satisfied with myself.

Sitting down at the desk, I began to scribble some notes about the women who had died. They had to have checked in today or yesterday, since it was now almost 2 a.m. Wow, that man, Mr. Kline, had gotten out of that room just in time.

The knock on the door shocked me out of my thoughts. It had to be Bea coming to get me.

"I'm ready if you..." No one was there. Again, I stretched my neck out, looking toward the fire escape then down toward the elevators. "What is it about me that makes this so much fun?" I shut the door quietly. Other people at the spa slept nicely in their beds with the lights off and nothing pulling itself out of the wallpaper or dropping down from an astral plane to suck out their life force like the juice of an orange slice.

Before I could get to the desk to sit back down, the knock came again.

I peeked out the peephole and saw nothing.

"I'm not opening for you."

Nothing but the room's heater kicking on made any noise. Tiptoeing back to the desk, I sat down just as the remote control for the television flew across the room, banging into the wall.

"Now you just stop that right now! If you cause any damage, I'm going to get stuck paying for it," I said, trying to sound brave.

Standing up, I realized that for the first time in my life, I felt like I didn't want to pursue this. But if something was watching me, I had to save face, right? As I reached down to pick up the remote, I saw my hand shaking so fast it looked like a blur. But my fingers worked, and I held it tightly while walking back to the desk.

Again the knock on the door.

"Did you invite friends?" My voice trembled. I walked over to the door. Just as I was about to peek out the peephole, I had a dreadful thought. What if I went to look and something looked back at me, something with sinister red or yellow eyes?

Show no fear. My thoughts sounded much braver than I was feeling, that was for sure. I got on tiptoe and looked at the peephole without putting my eye right on it. The light of the hallway was all that showed through. A deep breath came out that I hadn't even realized I was holding.

But no sooner had the hair on the back of my neck begun to relax than another earnest knocking came at the door. Three quick raps. Loud. Serious. I looked at the crack at the bottom of the door and saw that something was moving back and forth.

Images of the tentacles from the Prestwick house popped into my head, and a cold sweat coated me.

"That's nowhere near here," I mumbled to myself. "We put a lock on that place. Nothing is getting through. I checked it and double-checked it."

But I hadn't been myself for so long. What if I had missed something, and it got out? What if it had followed me here? My whole body began to shake, and I realized that if I didn't open that door and face whatever was on the other side, I might as well just lock myself away forever.

Swallowing hard, I stomped to the door, grabbed hold of the cold lever in my hot, sweaty hand, pushed it down, and yanked it open with such force that it banged against the little rubber nub protruding from the wall to prevent the door from doing damage when a crazy woman yanks it open.

Standing before me was something I was not prepared for.

Little Beastie

Can I come in?" Blake asked, his eyebrows pinched together as if I had somehow annoyed him by answering the door.

I stepped aside for him to enter and thought what a scandal it would have been at one time for a single lady to have a single man in her hotel room. What would Darla think? She might just call off their wedding if she ever were to find out he was behind closed doors at a health and wellness spa.

Wait! No one said they were getting married. I cleared my throat, wrapped my arms protectively around myself, and waited for him to speak.

"I've got a question to ask you."

I held my breath as he looked searchingly into my eyes. It made me feel self-conscious, like I was dressed up and my slip was showing or I had a run in my pantyhose.

"Okay." I shrugged. Did he even know why I was being so standoffish? Had Darla mentioned anything about how mean she had been to me in high school? Even if she told him with quivering lips and sad eyes, explaining how cruel *I* had been to *her* every day. Or did Blake just think I was the jealous type, acting hurt, all the while plotting revenge like Medea in that Greek tragedy?

It was funny that Medea had popped into my head. She was the only female character to not only set the wheels of murder in motion but to screw up big time, killing her own children instead of Jason's mistress, but still the gods hadn't punished her.

Of course they hadn't. Jason was a jerk. Medea had a few miles on her, sure. She wasn't the prettiest thing in the world, but she'd helped him get the golden fleece. She'd saved him from getting killed. But that wasn't good enough. Nope. Jason had to go and pick a woman so different from Medea it was like comparing a dandelion to a rose, and when he did this, it drove Medea insane. Why should she be punished when Blake drove her to do it?

No. Wait. Not Blake. Jason. I was thinking about

Jason in the old story, that low-down, dirty dog. Not the low-down, dirty dog in front of me.

"Are you all right?" Blake asked, his voice sharp like the clashing of cymbals.

I nodded.

"Just trying to remember a movie I saw. What did you need?" I thought I recovered quite well from that and didn't look like too much of a stuttering dunce.

"I said, did you happen to see the two sisters around the spa? They had just checked in. From what I have gathered so far, they dropped their things in the room and tried to cover the entire grounds within a couple hours."

Wrinkling my nose, I thought but had to shake my head. I couldn't be sure that I hadn't seen them. My head had been in such a haze that they might have walked right up to me, but I wouldn't have known it. But my gut assured me that our paths had not crossed.

He added, "A girl was murdered here during the Prohibition era before it was a hotel and spa and when it was a small shack doubling as a speakeasy and hideout for…unsavories."

"Interesting," I said, hiding my urge to ask questions. "But I think I heard Bea say all this was on the website. I mean, aside from the two girls who died today. The other death was common knowledge."

Even though I wanted to get involved in Blake's theory, even though my heart was breaking at the sight of him, I kept my distance and kept my spine straight, shoulders back, and gaze unflinching. Glancing at myself in the mirror, I was happy I appeared calm and indifferent, because inside I was like a room full of puppies fighting over one bone. Everything was being tugged in different directions, but no progress was being made in any.

I desperately wanted Blake to say something nice to me, something kind that I wouldn't have expected. But since it was obvious the conversation was going to focus on these two mysterious deaths, I gave up.

"Was it listed on the website that over the past ten years, there have been two other deaths on separate occasions?"

I wasn't sure I liked Blake's tone. If he had just come in here to lecture me on facts I had no knowledge of, this conversation was going to be pretty short.

"No, Blake. I didn't actually read anything about the place. Bea made all the arrangements. Maybe you should talk to her if you need those facts."

Hadn't the boys looked at the webpage? This sort of surprised me since Jake had said that he knew the spa was the party place for all things paranormal.

"What did Bea tell you?"

I got the feeling that Blake was stalling. The only time a guy did something like that was when he was trying to say something you didn't want to hear but couldn't find the right words or right time.

I repeated people's reports of seeing things move in their rooms and hearing knocking at the door when no one was there. Disembodied voices. But I left out the astral spiders and wild women who shape-shift. And it was a good thing I did.

"Those things are just publicity stunts," Blake said when I mentioned the online comments about the place. "Come on, Cath. You don't really believe in all that stuff. You are much too smart." Blake snickered as he took a seat at the desk and pulled out the little black leather pad all detectives seemed to use to write down their notes.

Suddenly I felt only two feet high.

Didn't Blake remember? Hadn't the Prestwick house impressed itself in his head like it had in mine? Didn't it haunt him and stare back at him in all its horrific glory from shadows in dreams and in reality? Could something be attached to him, feeding off him, like what had been on me?

"But Blake, how can you say that? Don't you remember—"

"The ordeal at the property? I remember your storming in to play amateur detective and lousing up a crime scene. Then bringing your whole family to do more of the same."

His words held such bite that I couldn't help but wince.

"You know, Cath, I understand it's trendy and hip to be different, to be unique, to even be something you are not. But you and your aunt need to get a better grip on reality. Otherwise there may come a day when someone with authority overhears you and decides you're too great a risk to society, locks you both up, and throws away the key."

I couldn't stop myself.

"But you were there. You saw all the—"

"I didn't see a damn thing, Cath. Nothing at all happened at that house except for you contaminating the scene. Jake will back me up on this."

Jake? This made me feel like I was in that movie with the people being taken over by pods. Jake wouldn't flip on us. Not on his own family. He certainly wouldn't do anything that would hurt Bea.

All you had to do was see them together and you'd know he wouldn't betray her gift. Not for money or fame or even to appease his weirdo partner.

Blake was wrong. Dead wrong. I watched him as he stared into his little leather notebook.

"Then what did you come to my room for, Blake?" My voice sounded like a china teacup that had fallen onto a hard ceramic floor.

"I had a couple theories I wanted to go over with you. Those sisters who died had no other family. They were orphans. Their mother and father died under curious circumstances."

I thought of my own mother. Of course I did. But Blake didn't know anything about her. He didn't know anything about me, but it was pretty obvious he had already formed an opinion that was none too flattering. Yet here he was in my room asking for advice.

"I think they committed suicide," he continued. "The markings on their skin look like symptoms of arsenic poisoning."

I said nothing. The words I wanted to speak had jammed between my head and my heart, and nothing but a couple peculiar chokes came out.

"But the odd thing was that their lips and fingertips were blue, and that is a symptom of cyanosis."

He didn't look at me and instead stared at the wood-grain design of the desk.

I couldn't move. It was as if I was surrounded by a swarm of hornets and didn't dare move for fear of getting stung. But my mind was whirling wildly with thoughts, ideas, comments, and emotions all flashing at super speed but not long enough for me to hold on to a single one.

"You need to leave," I blurted.

That got his attention. He looked up at me as if I had just burped out loud.

"You do. You don't need me for this. I'd like to go to bed. Not play detective."

Slowly and deliberately, Blake stood up from the desk, tucked his notebook back into his inside pocket, straightened his tie, and headed toward the door, shaking his head.

"You don't have to be so sensitive. You just need to remember when you make a mistake, you fix it, or you make sure you never do it again. You don't dream up a bunch of circumstances to cover up your mistake."

It was a brief hesitation. If I hadn't been staring at Blake with disbelief, I would have missed it. But there it was: a flash of reluctance during which I thought maybe he would stop, turn around, say something nice, something soft to restore my hope that maybe he was hiding feelings for me. But he pulled the door open, stepped out, and let it fall shut on its own without so much as a good-bye or good-night or kiss my ass.

That was it. I was alone. I shivered.

"Pull yourself together, Cath," I mumbled to my reflection. "You've got a fine fellow who wants to take you for dinner. If nothing else, maybe he'll be a good guy you can call if there is a spider in the tub or that light bulb you can't reach in the hallway goes out."

I walked to my balcony. Pulling the curtain aside, I remembered the little bird that had died out there. Quickly I pulled the heavy door open and stepped onto the platform, looking around to where I had seen him, but I saw nothing.

Letting out a long sigh, I felt relief that the little beastie must have just stunned itself. I double-checked and found no feathers, no ants, no nothing. He had to have come to and flown off. Good. Good.

Funny how that gave me hope just as Blake Samberg had tried to take it all away from me. Maybe he was more compatible with Darla after all. Or maybe she had gotten to him as I suspected she might have, feeding him her version of things and glossing over or leaving out her own contribution to my pain and suffering.

"Tom Warner seems nice," I said out loud, as if that might make the words more convincing.

But he isn't Blake.

"Who cares?" I gritted my teeth. "Blake Samberg thinks I should be locked up and that I'm crazy. If only he knew what I could have done to him just then! I could have torn his voice right from his throat! I could have paralyzed him from the waist down! I could have made him think he was drowning in the middle of the room! All of this without even laying a finger on him!" These words came out of my mouth hot and final.

"If he knew that, maybe he would have thought twice before being so cruel. If he was scared of the Prestwick house, he'd really have something to fear if only he knew what I could do."

Maybe he already did.

The thought was a lead weight across my shoulders. Could it be he was being so mean because he was scared of me? Didn't he see that I had gone there to save him? I would never have hurt him or let anything else hurt him, not as long as I had use of my arms and breath in my lungs.

Suddenly Darla's petty comments didn't seem so

important. Gosh, could I have been so spiteful, so vindictive as to hurt the man I lo...to hurt Blake because my nose had been tweaked?

Taking a deep breath, I looked out into the night. The grounds beneath the balcony looked cool and creepy at the same time. The spots illuminated by the little solar lights glowed in a rainbow of colors, and strategically placed floodlights illuminated thick, tall trees. The wind blew just a little, and I heard the far-off call of an owl.

Hearing an owl meant someone was going to die. Or they already had.

Crime Scene

✦❀✦

It wasn't long after Blake had left my room that the telephone rang. The electronic beeping sent me to the ceiling in surprise. Before I could even say hello, I heard Bea's voice.

"It's time. Meet me out back."

"Got it."

CLICK.

Quickly I slipped my feet into the rubber-soled footies that Bea had picked up for me and a hoodie that was more white than gray, but it was the only thing that would keep me warm and hide my face.

If I knew Bea, she was getting a little exercise by taking the stairs. I opted for the elevator. No one was up at this hour with the exception of the occupants of one room, the quiet murmur of whose television came pulsing through their door. Even my feet, covered in these soft slip-ons, could be heard making the faintest pat-pat-pat with each step.

I looked behind me. I was still alone in the hallway but was relieved when I got to the elevator bank, pressed the button, and heard the ping of the available elevator almost instantly.

The doors slid open, and I stepped inside. I thought of Aunt Astrid blending into the lovely tapestry and wondered what she had been up to in her early days that she'd had to do the same trick. I looked at my reflection in the doors and then glanced at the number, which had remained on three.

Had I forgotten to punch the G button on the panel? Maybe. I pushed it and heard the sound of cables and motors kicking into gear.

What was I afraid of? I was alone in the elevator.

As if on cue, the lights went out. The elevator continued to move, but I was in the most pitch-black darkness ever.

I instantly reached in front of me, fumbling across the button panel. How long could this take? The place had only three floors. I tried to feel for the button that would alert the front desk in the event of an emergency. Where was it? How many floors was I going down? How long had I been in this box? Panic was seizing my heart, and pretty soon I was convinced that when those doors finally opened, I'd be staring at a river of fire surrounded by jagged-edged cliffs and mountains with deformed creatures holding pitchforks, dancing around the flames and reaching for me.

Where was that panic button? It was as if it had been removed or covered. I slid my hands over the buttons, saying in my head *third floor, second floor, ground floor*, but no matter how far down my hands went, I found nothing else on that panel.

My pupils stretched, trying to grab some shred of light, but I could see nothing. And that deep pit in the back of my mind, the one that held the images of those hands reaching out from underneath my bed to get my mother, snapped into crystal-clear focus. I was suddenly frozen with fear. Just because I didn't see anything didn't mean something wasn't watching me.

With that thought, I felt a cold, slimy texture slide over my bare ankle.

I had just opened my mouth to scream when the light flickered back on as the doors slid open to reveal the lobby. I ran out of the elevator, not caring what I looked like or who noticed me. I dove out of there, walking quickly backward, keeping my eyes on that open, sinister maw until I was sure nothing was going to come out and drag me back inside. The doors slowly slid shut as if they were waiting for me to change my mind and climb back aboard.

I'd be taking the stairs with Bea from now on. I could use the exercise.

Fumbling and worrying my key-card, the only thing I had in my pocket, I felt good being out in the open. The sky was still black, but a very hazy twilight was fooling with my eyes in the east. The sun would be up in a little while. Normally that made a person feel better, like they had made it through the worst of the terror. I wasn't so convinced of that at the moment.

Circling around the grounds to the back of the building, I slowed my steps and looked around.

"Bea!" I said in the loudest whisper I could muster.

"Here!" she called back from behind a clump of bushes that I hoped didn't have thorns on them. Looking around quickly, I dashed for the shrub.

"This reminds me of when we played ghost in the graveyard as kids," I said, taking her hand in mine and squeezing it tightly.

"I was thinking that exact same thing," she said. I could hear the smile in her voice.

"Do we know which room your mom is in?"

"I'm pretty sure it's that one with the curtains parted just a little."

Scanning the terrain, I realized that this room was located next to the mosaic wall that Olga had talked about.

"You won't believe what happened to me in the elevator." My eyes wouldn't leave the mosaic tiles, but they remained still and beautiful.

"Oh yeah? What happened?"

Curtains rustled, the balcony door slid open, and a hand that looked detached from a body waved in our direction.

"There's Mom." We hadn't let go of each other's hands and ran like two girls on their way to kindergarten as the bell rang.

The terror I had felt in the elevator gave way to a feeling of exhilaration. As usual, being with my family made me feel more confident, and Blake's words, although they still stung, started to settle.

Telling Bea what he'd said would have caused unnecessary stress between her and Jake. No cop wants to hear his partner be called a grade-A jerk. Plus, it wasn't as if Jake could do anything to change his mind. Blake thought I was crazy, and that was all there was to it. Right now I had to focus on my family and whatever we were going to find in that room.

Quietly we pulled ourselves up onto the balcony platform and swung our legs over the railing. Within a matter of seconds, we were inside the room.

"You guys aren't going to believe this. There is so much going on in this room that I am surprised there hasn't been an incident every couple of days," Aunt Astrid said, holding the curtains aside as we snuck in. She slid the door closed, and I heard the lock snap into place. She was still thoroughly blending in with the environment, but if I looked hard enough, I could see her eyes.

"Let the veil be lifted and the flower bloom," she muttered to herself, and suddenly her lovely, familiar face came into view.

"What if someone comes in?" I asked, pointing to the front door.

"Don't worry. I've slipped the hook into place. They'll get the door open a crack. Just enough time for you guys to hustle out of here. Then I'll open it and slip out right under their noses." Aunt Astrid giggled. "Now, come. Let's get this started."

Before I took a seat on the floor between my aunt and cousin, I looked around the room. For a crime scene, it held very little indication that anyone had even been in the room. The beds were still made. The suitcases were there, but they were closed. Perhaps the deceased sisters had left toiletries and bits of clothing in the bathroom; I couldn't see from here. But nothing looked disturbed at all.

I took a seat, and we all joined hands.

"Mom, it feels weird in here," Bea whispered, tightening her grip on my hand.

"There is a lot of sadness in this room, honey," Aunt Astrid said as she let go of my hand and pointed. An open space separated the mirror and the desk. Following her finger, I looked at the pretty blue-and-white–patterned wallpaper until a set of pitch-black eyes snapped open.

Shadow Man

❧❧

Bea must have seen them at the same time since her grip became like a vise on my hand. Stepping out from the wall was a petite woman. Even though she had the flower-and-paisley print of the wallpaper all over her, it was obvious she was from a different era.

Her hair fell in loose finger waves. Her dress looked like a simple thing that a young woman might wear to church. I didn't see her feet, as they faded into nothingness. But she was wringing her hands nervously.

The woman didn't smile. She kept looking toward the sliding door as if expecting someone to enter that way.

"We're here to help you, dear. What is your name?" Aunt Astrid asked. She had a way with the spirits, as her many accurate fortunetelling sessions at the Brew-Ha-Ha would attest.

The lips of the blue and white, paisley and flowered woman moved, but neither Bea nor I could hear a sound. But my aunt listened intently, nodding and clicking her tongue.

"Sadie. Sadie McGill is my name," Aunt Astrid began. *"I'm waiting for my boyfriend, Waldo Ferguson."*

Listening to my aunt and observing the strange apparition was like watching a badly dubbed movie.

"Waldo was a wonderful man," Sadie/Aunt Astrid said apologetically. *"It was just that he was married. Oh yes, I knew it was wrong. But the way he looked at me the first time we met, I knew he was the man for me. Even if my sister had seen him first, had brought him home to meet our parents, and I had been her maid of honor."*

My jaw hit the floor. This couldn't be the only thing haunting this spa, could it? A brokenhearted dame who managed to have an affair with her sister's husband? By the looks of Sadie McGill, she didn't seem all that intimidating.

"Waldo was supposed to meet me here tonight. He was breaking things off with my sister, and we were going to leave. He had a cousin in Chicago who would give him a job. We could start over away from the scandal. No one would judge us there. But…he is late."

I looked at Bea out of the corner of my eye and squeezed her hand in mine. I didn't need Sadie to finish her tale of woe. I knew where this was going. Just then she looked nervously toward the balcony door.

"I'm afraid. Every night I hear the laughing and scratching along the walls and the ceiling. Strange people come into this room, and they can't help me. They won't help me."

Bea's hand tightened around mine.

"And the shadows don't ever stop." She looked at the three of us, but her lips didn't move. Looking toward the balcony again, she began to tremble and cry.

"No. No, Waldo. You don't mean it. You don't mean those things."

A dark shadow as thick as ink wafted into the room as if it bloomed from a corner. It hovered over Sadie, and she looked up at it in love and fear. She began to shake her head, still kneading her hands. Aunt Astrid had stopped interpreting the conversation. We could obviously see what was going on. Waldo wasn't leaving his wife, Sadie's sister. But Sadie wasn't going to make it out of this room.

She turned from the shadow, uttering a scream that only she could hear, her face contorted into a grimace of pain from the heart and from the shadow that all but consumed her. Her hands went to her throat, clawing and pulling at the misty hands that had encircled it.

Unlike the other guests who had seen Sadie run out of the wallpaper, we stayed still and saw the shadow take hold of her.

Within minutes, her body went limp, and she and the shadow disappeared.

"Did you all see that? You saw that, right? It wasn't just me." I was always so worried I was hallucinating. No matter how many years I'd been a practicing witch, there were some gifts that I never got used to. Seeing the dead when they still thought they were living was one of them.

"She called that shadow man Waldo," Bea said. "Is he the one killing people in this room?"

"Waldo is still alive. That is why we can only see his shadow. She is reliving her death because no matter what he has done, she loves him. She'd rather see him as the last thing she sees in life than go on without him in death." Aunt Astrid wiped a single tear from her eye.

"Is that normal? I mean, is that what love is? Because I'm not so sure that should be what love is." I had forgotten to keep my voice down and scooted so my back could rest against the bed.

"None of this is normal. And no, Waldo is not what is killing people. Like Sadie said, there are things in this place. We should have known with the astral spiders being so prevalent. No, something else is going on here. Waldo had just succumbed to it."

Bea stood up and sat down on the bed next to me. I was glad she did. The heebie-jeebies were starting, and even the simple feeling of her leg next to my shoulder made me feel safer. Aunt Astrid scooted along the floor and rested her back against the other bed.

"No. We've stumbled upon something much bigger here."

"Well, whatever it is isn't just in this room." My voice was almost mad. I explained what had happened with the knocks on my door and the elevator. I also mentioned the woman I had seen running and Olga's story.

"Add that on top of the astral spiders, and I hope you guys don't mind if I don't let you plan any more vacations for me." I stood up and stretched, still looking around for anything out of the ordinary and remembering not just one but two women had died here, two young women. Three if you wanted to include Sadie.

"I think Sadie was the first," Aunt Astrid said. "She triggered something."

"What makes you say that, Mom?"

"If this place had suspicious deaths on a regular basis, it would have gone out of business. But a death here and there, every couple of years, even decades, no one would pay much attention to. Blake already said he was sure it was a suicide. Maybe it was. But why here and why tonight?"

"Do you think it could be a ritual killing?" I couldn't believe the words coming out of my mouth, but there they were.

"Some serial killers lie dormant for that long until the need arises."

"So are we dealing with some paranormal serial killer? Good luck figuring out how to stop that," I griped.

"No." Aunt Astrid put up her hand. "I think if we looked into the history, we'd see that the deaths came at certain times. We just need to figure out what those times have in common. And once we know that, I'll bet they point us in the direction of who is responsible."

"That is going to take a good bit of digging, and we check out the day after tomorrow," Bea said.

"Call me crazy, but I don't want to stay in this

place any longer than we have to." I rubbed my hands together. "I'm tired of knocks on the door, and I don't think I'll ever ride an elevator again, plus—"

The door banged open, catching on the metal hook Aunt Astrid had put into place. We all froze.

"What the hell, Baker? Get the door open."

"I'm trying. The lock is on it."

"How can that be? That would have to be locked from the inside, and there ain't nobody inside."

"Well, I can't get it." Baker closed the door and tried it a second time. Again it caught on the safety latch.

Bea and I jumped up and hurried to the balcony door. I pulled the curtains aside and just as quickly pulled them shut again.

"Jake is out there!" I hissed.

Bea rolled her eyes and tossed her head back in disbelief.

"Of all the rotten luck." She looked at her mom. "What do we do?"

"There isn't time. Get under the beds."

"They'll check under there," I argued.

"They probably already have. Now hurry."

We had no choice. The wolves were at the door.

It was a tight squeeze for both of us, but we managed to get underneath the beds. Aunt Astrid, still blending in almost seamlessly with her surroundings, made her way toward the door. I heard the squeak of the latch being unhooked and hoped she had enough sense to step out of the way, because Baker and his partner were probably going to use a good bit of force.

I was right.

The door banged open with such force that it shook the floor. Part of me wanted to reach out and pull up the dust ruffle just enough to peek out, but the other part of me didn't want to get caught, so I just listened.

What if these guys were going to be in here for hours? How were we going to get out of this mess? Why didn't we leave and discuss the facts outside?

"There, see. It was just stuck a little," Baker said to his partner.

"Well, snap on the light. I'm not going in there when it is pitch black."

"What's the matter, Kowalski, scared?"

"Hey, I don't know about you, but I've heard stories about this place. I'm not taking any chances."

"Yeah, I heard the stories, too. A suicide here, a homicide there. People getting lost, drowning in the hot springs. It's just a coincidence. Who knows what kind of recreational 'herbs' some of these people are on. I'll bet if we did a drug sweep, we'd make a pretty good bust," Baker said, sitting down on my side of the bed, pushing the box spring into my head. I cringed. Where was Aunt Astrid?

"Are you really that much of an ignoramus?" Kowalski said. "This is one of those all-natural places. I don't even think they cook meat in this place."

They don't, I screamed in my head.

Suddenly a loud crash could be heard coming from the lobby. Both officers jumped.

"What the hell?"

"It has got to be a full moon tonight. Let's go."

They took off running out of the room. The pressure was off my head, and I scrambled out from under the bed in time to help Bea to her feet.

Aunt Astrid stood awkwardly at the door, fading in and out of view.

"Quickly! Out and onto the elevator."

I froze.

"Can't we take the stairs?" My body began to shudder.

"If you take the stairs, you'll have to go past the lobby, and those men will be heading back any second. Quick! To the elevator!"

Bea grabbed my hand and dragged me out of the

room toward the elevator. It was standing there open. Had Aunt Astrid left it open for us? Or was it like a baby with its mouth open, waiting for more food?

With one good yank, Bea had me inside. She pressed the number three button and started the doors sliding closed. I held onto her like a drowning woman would hold a life preserver. My eyes were squeezed shut. I heard her saying encouraging words and petting my hand like I was a child getting a shot. Within seconds, we were on the third floor, doors wide open, standing in the hallway, and I could breathe again.

"You poor thing," Bea said as she pulled her key card from her pocket. "Want to stay in my room tonight?"

"Oh, like a four-year-old scared of the dark? You bet your bippy I do." I had surrendered my pride over an hour ago.

"Good, because I didn't want to sleep alone either."

Minutes later, Aunt Astrid appeared at the top of the stairs.

Her body was back to normal except for her feet, which were the red, orange, and gold pattern of the rug, giving her the appearance of floating.

Bea held the door open, and I quickly made my way inside. Aunt Astrid followed and Bea brought up the rear, shutting the door, snapping the deadbolt, and flipping the safety lock like her mom had done in room 116.

"That was too close. Jake would have skinned me alive if he knew we were in there. Did you get away okay, Mom? That was you that made that crash, right?"

"Yes, it was me, and you aren't going to believe what I heard those two officers talking about when they came back."

Aunt Astrid stretched out on the closest bed, her feet finally turning back to their own fleshy color.

"This double suicide—at least that is what they are calling it—was not the first suicide of siblings in this place." She began to yawn. We had been up all day, and the sun would be rising in a couple hours. "According to Kowalski, when he first started in the state police department about fifteen years ago, two sisters died here."

"Let me guess. Did they stay in room 116?" I was sure I knew the answer.

"No. They went out into the grounds and shot themselves. I don't mean one killed the other and then herself. They both had pistols and both killed themselves. No word of an argument, of any dispute. They had no parents and no next of kin. Strange, right?"

I couldn't help but think that Bea and I had escaped something by the skin of our teeth. When I looked at her, I wanted to cry.

"I know what you're thinking, Cath," she said, looking back at me. "We are so much like sisters that maybe it could have just as easily been us. Right?"

Slowly I nodded.

Bea rushed over to me, and we sat on the other bed, holding hands. She tried to smooth my hair, but suddenly I felt very angry.

"What kind of a thing preys on the bond between two kids? That is really just plain sick."

"It is very disturbing," Aunt Astrid said, her eyes heavy but still clear. "We need to rest now. Tomorrow, I say we venture into town for an early breakfast and see what the locals can tell us."

Bea patted my leg to stand up, and we pulled the blankets back, climbing in and sharing the bed like we had so many nights growing up. Aunt Astrid took the other bed for herself. None of us wanted to be alone. I looked at the digital clock. It read 2:45 a.m.

If we slept until seven, that would be enough. We could sleep under our facials and in the mud bath and hot spring soaks, too. We'd probably need it after going into town.

As I let my shoulders sink into the mattress and my head became snuggled into the pillow, I realized that I hadn't felt this safe or this comfortable since we had gotten here. Family was what did it. It wasn't the smell of lavender and sage everywhere. It wasn't the down pillows or perfectly monitored room temperatures. It was having my family here. I fell into a deep sleep within seconds.

When I awoke, I had an idea. I couldn't remember a dream leading me to it or a visit from some paranormal good Samaritan. But it was there, and like Blake Samberg always said, you go with a hunch.

Green Aura

❧

Mo's Grill was a rustic-looking place set dead in the center of the little area of unincorporated Wonder Falls. When we walked in I was almost knocked over by the captivating smell of crackling, crispy bacon.

"Thank goodness we decided to come here," I said to my aunt as we all moseyed up to the counter. The dining room was bustling with early risers, coffee cups were steaming, silverware was clanking, and the constant tune of conversations all mixed together topped it off.

We took our seats, and I wasted no time grabbing a tiny menu. Within two seconds of glancing down the list of items, I had made my decision.

"I am so hungry." I rubbed my stomach as I spoke.

"Me too," Bea said.

A broad-shouldered, baggy-eyed waitress with stringy brown hair pulled into a ponytail stood behind the counter, wiping her hands on her apron. She yelled to the cook.

"You got those two dots and a dash for me yet?" She looked at the three of us, rolling her eyes. "I'll be right with you, ladies. Coffee?"

We all nodded enthusiastically.

From behind the counter separating the kitchen from the rest of the diner popped a shiny head with a few short remnants of black hair around the ears and a thick black mustache. He delivered a steaming white plate that the waitress quickly scooped up and hustled to another table.

She came back to us, straightening her Harley-Davidson T-shirt, wiping her hands on her apron again then pulling out her order pad.

"Got a fresh pot brewing. What can I get you ladies?"

I ordered a bacon burger with everything on it and french fries. My aunt got a cheese omelet, and Bea ordered herself a full stack of blueberry pancakes.

Our waitress nodded, tore off the receipt, tucked it into the carousel on the counter, and spun it toward the cook before banging the little bell.

"Order!"

She hurried off and returned within seconds with hot coffees and water. With the pot still in her hand, she swung around the counter to offer refills to everyone else in the place.

"I think we ought to bend this waitress's ear when we get a chance. She looks like she's been around for a while and might have some information. I'll bet over the years, other guests from the spa have come here," Bea said.

We sipped our coffee for a few minutes until my aunt dropped a comment that stopped my blood cold and almost made me lose my appetite. Almost.

"So, you never did say anything about Officer Tom Warner. How did you meet that tall drink of water?"

Bea leaned on her elbow and batted her eyes in my direction.

Stuttering like Porky Pig, I just blurted out the truth.

"Well, there are stranger ways to meet a fellow than that. He made a special trip all the way to the spa to make sure you were okay. That was very sweet," Bea added.

"And from what I could see, he had never been married and also had an exciting green aura."

"A green aura?"

"A green aura? Oh, that is rare. You might want to take a longer look at this guy, Cath." Bea took a sip of her coffee and batted her eyelashes again over the cup.

"You know, you may think this is all fun and games, but we've got a serious issue on our hands at the spa. There is no time for romance."

"There is always time for romance," Bea insisted. "Especially if you are going to be married to a cop."

"Married? The guy just asked me to dinner."

"He did? Well, that's wonderful. When are you going?" Aunt Astrid patted my arm.

"I'll help you pick out an outfit," Bea added.

"Heads up, ladies," the waitress said just in time.

Finally, with good, old-fashioned comfort food in front of us, the next fifteen minutes went by in almost complete silence, with the exception of a few *hm-hms* and *yums*.

That bacon burger went down as if I were a woman on death row enjoying her final meal. We were all quite full. We patted our bellies, ordered another round of coffee, and waited for things to die down so we could interrogate the waitress about the spa.

"The Muskox? Oh yeah." She rolled her tongue like she had a piece of food stuck in one of her back teeth. Her eyes narrowed a little. "Yeah, I've heard the stories. Just about everyone in town has. Most everyone here steers clear of the place."

"Why is that?" Aunt Astrid asked. This waitress was not as old as she looked. Years of getting by on a waitress's salary can be hard on a lady sometimes. Add a biker lifestyle, which I was pretty sure this woman lived based on the tattoo on her arm that peeked out from the short sleeve ("Born to Ride, Oddie and Maureen 1987 Daytona"), and I believed it was safe to assume she had been around the block a few times.

"Well, there are a couple reasons. One, the SOBs who run the place deliberately instruct people to come in via the long route, avoiding I-80 and the town. We got nice businesses here and decent folks and could use the business the spa brings in." She leaned on the counter in front of all three of us, and we instinctively leaned in closer to her. "Personally, I think it's that greedy disposition that brings so much bad luck to the place."

"Bad luck?" Bea prodded.

"Just last night, another suicide occurred."

"News travels fast," I said, nodding.

"Yeah. When it comes to the Muskox, it does. About six years ago, there was another double suicide. Two women. We heard they had gone crazy or something and went running outside, stark naked and raving mad, and they shot themselves."

It was only natural that some of the details would change, bend, or stretch just a little in any town when being relayed from neighbor to neighbor. But the gist was still the same.

"And before that, two children disappeared. Hey, Bob?" She turned around to the cook in the kitchen, who popped up, his balding head sweating. "How old were those kids who went missing up at Spooky Spa?"

He scratched his dome.

"Had to be about fifteen, sixteen years old if I remember right," he said then lowered his head. Steam rose from where he was and a thick, hairy hand reached up, grabbed an empty plate, and pulled it out of view to the other side of the counter.

"Yeah. They found those kids about four days later. Said they wandered off the trail and got lost.

Died from the elements. So they say." She patted my aunt's hand for a second and gave us all a wink. "One second. Duty calls."

Maureen turned, grabbed the coffee pot and the plate from under the red heating lamp, and made the rounds to the handful of remaining patrons. When she came back, she had more to say.

"Now you tell me how two kids that age, healthy and normal by all accounts, can get lost and die in four days? I happen to know for a fact, too, that they had strange markings on them. Like they had died of choking or something."

It had to be the blue lips she was referring to. I didn't look at my family, but I knew we were all thinking the same thing.

"Has anyone ever spoken to the owners, the mayor, the people of the town to try and find out what is going on?" Bea asked.

"Nope."

"Why don't they?" Sipping my coffee, I barely noticed how hot it was as I followed Maureen's story.

"I can't say for sure. There are only rumors."

"What kind of rumors?" Aunt Astrid was watching the woman closely.

"Now, I can't say this is fact for sure. But there are a lot of people who claim to believe that the place is somehow cursed."

"Cursed?" I rolled my eyes as if that was the most outlandish, far-fetched theory ever concocted and second only to the Kennedy assassination magic bullet and the hoax of the moon landing.

"Right?" she agreed with me. "This is what I've heard. The land used to belong to the Wyandot Indian tribe. They have since become extinct, but way back when, a gentleman by the name of Chief Big Running Fox was in charge of a good piece of land they had occupied. Well, he had his eye on some young woman from a neighboring tribe. She had a sister or a twin or something. So, the chiefs spoke and the girl's father said if Chief Big Running Fox gave his land to the other tribe, he could have his daughter."

We were all enthralled. I sipped my coffee, waiting for the rest of the local history lesson.

"So Chief Big Running Fox took the deal. He got the daughter and handed over his land. Well, he didn't know that the other tribe had made a deal with some white folks to buy that land. The other tribe was given actual silver, and Chief Big Running

Fox's tribe began to slowly starve, including the daughter of the other chief."

"Well for pete's sake," Aunt Astrid mumbled.

"When Chief Big Running Fox found this out, he cursed his land. Said it would be the most soothing, beautiful, bountiful land under the stars but that anyone settling on it would suffer immeasurable losses. Just to add insult to injury, the young lady killed herself along with her sister because they were both so ashamed of their menfolk. And since I've been here, which is over forty years now, every couple of years, that story surfaces with another tragedy at that place."

A customer from afar dropped a fork, causing all of us to jump.

"You can bet no one from town goes there. Not anyone who has roots in this town. Not anyone with a family," she added and folded her arms over her saggy bosom. "From what we've heard here in town, the family that started the place died out, and now it is run by some kind of board or trust or some other anonymous Mr. Moneybags. And it has been years, maybe even over a decade, since someone from the estate came to check on the place. The whole thing is weird."

"Has anyone from around here ever worked at the place?" Aunt Astrid asked.

"No one that I know of," Maureen huffed. "But from what I've seen and heard, the place must pay the staff pretty well, because they rarely ever come into town, and if they do, mum's the word. For all I know, they are cursed, too."

Woogie-Boogie Hullaballoo

❧❦❧

"Cursed land doesn't make sense with the victims. Not with the suicides and the siblings and all that," I squawked as we drove back toward the Muskox.

"No. It doesn't. What about the relatively calm years in between? The business isn't struggling. It is thriving. That doesn't sound cursed to me either," Bea said as she maneuvered the car through the narrow streets of unincorporated Wonder Falls.

"Well, if it is cursed land, yet it isn't doing anything but claiming a couple of victims every few years, then that sounds like…"

"A sacrifice!" It was like I'd answered the Final Jeopardy question.

"A sacrifice." Aunt Astrid nodded. "Now that finally makes some sense. But now we have to find out the who, what, and when of all that in order to tell us what we can do to stop it. If only I had my books."

"Right. Next time we take a vacation for a few days, we'll just rent a U-Haul for at least half of your library in case we stumble into a random woogie-boogie hullaballoo," I teased.

"Wait. If we are dealing with a Native American jinx, then we have to remember how they would have looked at things. The days, the seasons, the time were all calculated using the stars and the sun and moon," Bea said, blinking wildly. "I'll bet if we trace back the dates of the last couple of suicides, we'll find a correlation with the stars."

"And how are we going to do that?" The last thing I wanted to do was spend the whole day in a library.

"First, I am going to search the Internet in the hospitality room. It shouldn't be hard to get the history of deaths at the spa or the lunar schedule for those days. Then we are going to go for our facials, mud baths, and hot spring soaks," Bea said.

"But then what?" I thought about the elevator the previous night and wondered if that was part of the Indian curse as well. It had to be. I didn't want to imagine that the Prestwick house had found me.

"Then we find a pattern and see what we can do to put an end to this curse."

When we got back to the hotel, my stomach was happy to have something other than leafy green stuff in it, and I was feeling quite good.

"I'm going to take a walk," Aunt Astrid said as we piled out of the car.

"Do you want me to go with you?" I wasn't scared now that the sun was up. I was nervous but not scared. There was a difference.

"No, honey. Why don't you go get yourself a smoothie or something and relax. This really was supposed to be a trip for you."

"I am right as rain." I flexed my biceps.

The smile that spread across my aunt's face made me feel twenty pounds of guilt.

"I was so hard on you, Aunt Astrid. I'm sorry for the trouble. I still can't believe I had that thing on me. You and Bea have no idea how much better I am feeling and how much, well, you know."

"Yeah, I know." She hugged me tightly and kissed my cheek. "Now, I'm going for a walk. If I'm not back in my room within an hour, ninety minutes tops, tell Jake and Blake and get the cavalry searching."

"Are you afraid you're going to see something? Something dangerous?"

"Forewarned is forearmed, Cath. Always be prepared."

"Just like the Boy Scouts." I gave my aunt a wink and headed into the spa.

Bea had already made a mad dash to the hospitality room to get on the computer and begin her research. She was always so good at that kind of stuff. In high school, the good grades came easily for her. She absorbed even the worst subjects like math and social studies, and the information just stuck in her head.

I sauntered into the lobby thinking I might get an hour of sleep or at least an episode of my favorite crime show on the tube before getting my face slathered with sea kelp or red clay. But before I could get to the stairs—you can bet I wasn't setting foot in the elevator—I found myself a comfy seat in a corner, my back against the wall, with a view of the whole place.

It *was* a very tranquil place. The lighting, the mellow music, and the soothing colors made it very relaxing to just sit and watch the people, the staff. I wondered if this place was run on a trust or by a board of directors, who paid the staff? Who was in charge here?

Standing up and stretching my legs, I went to talk to the tall guy pacing behind the front desk like a manager. But before I got to him, I saw a figure coming toward me that I wasn't prepared for at all.

"Hey, Cath," Jake said, waving to me. His face was crinkled with worry.

"Hi, Jake. What's shakin'?"

"Have you seen Bea?"

"She was just a couple steps ahead of me. I think she was going to her room to do something. Burn some sage, maybe, to get into the proper frame of mind for our facials. You know Bea. Everything has a ritual to make it special." I shrugged and smiled. I didn't want to send him to the hospitality suite to catch Bea scouring the web for the history of this place and the Native American folklore plus lunar schedules for the past half century. He'd instantly know we were up to something.

"That's okay. Actually, I'd like to talk to you."

"Me?" My cousin's husband was like a brother to me, and we'd had plenty of conversations, serious discussions, and even a debate or two. But he never really spoke to me when he was working on a case, especially if it was giving him the heebie-jeebies.

"Okay. Do you want to sit or go somewhere private or…?"

"Let's just walk."

I nodded, thrust my hands into my pockets, and waited for Jake to point us in whatever direction he wanted to go.

"Where is Blake?"

"He's still interviewing the last few folks who were on staff last night."

Again, I nodded since I wasn't really sure what else to do.

"So, what's this all about, Jake?"

He swallowed hard. I could tell that he was trying to figure out what words to use. Finally, he decided to just spill it.

"I saw something last night."

Drums

All I could think was that Jake had seen Aunt Astrid blending into the wallpaper or maybe Bea and me pulling ourselves up and over the balcony. I held my breath.

Jake looked around as if someone might hear him and two guys in white coats with butterfly nets were going to pop up from around the corner and snatch him up like a monarch.

"Saw something?" I acted dumb. It wasn't hard. "Something like a clue or tip or something like strange lights in the sky or a floating apparition?"

Jake chuckled nervously.

"No. I saw something…"

"Where was Blake? Did he see anything?"

"He had gone to the car to get a set of fresh rubber gloves. He seemed to be gone a long time."

Had that been the time he was up in my room? Did he lie to Jake about where he was going? I wasn't even good enough for him to say he wanted to talk to me? Too embarrassed, I guess. My ego sulked.

"The bodies had long been gone by this time," he started. "Those two women were from Glendale Heights, Montana."

"Yikes. They are a long way from home. Or should I say *were*." I grimaced. Jake didn't seem to be paying much attention to me. He was reliving whatever he had seen.

"I was just going through their room. The luggage. The drawers." Sweat started to form on his temples. I put my hand on his shoulder. "It was like I had blacked out for a few seconds. Maybe it was minutes. I'm not sure. But I sort of snapped out of it, and I was standing in the middle of the room, just staring at the curtains."

He shook as a shiver chased over his shoulders.

"I heard something."

Scratching? Growling? Heavy breathing? My mind jumped feet first into Terror-land. If it were anything like the elevator, I'd be sweating too.

"What did you hear?"

"Drums."

I cocked my head. Not at all what I had been thinking.

"Drums? What? Like marching drums?"

"No." Jake swallowed. "Like drums you'd hear before battle. Drums to scare the opposition, you know? They were pounding, pounding in a beat, and I could feel myself slipping into a trance again. Like I was being hypnotized or something."

"Geez, Jake."

"So I walked out in the hallway to see if I could hear them out there. And I could but not the same way. So I came back into the room and walked to the curtain. I could still hear them. I pulled the curtain aside, unlocked the sliding door, and leaned my head outside. I could hear them there, too. But…"

"But what?"

Jake slipped his hand under my arm, and we walked to the seat I had been sitting on just a few minutes earlier. We sat down next to each other, and he looked at me. But it wasn't me he was seeing. He was seeing past me into something that he didn't like.

"The sound was inside my head. And when I looked outside, I saw something in the trees."

I gulped. I hoped he wouldn't tell me he saw spiders.

"At first I thought it was just a trick of the light. It was dark while we were investigating, right? I felt a little bit of a breeze. Maybe I just imagined the whole thing?"

He seemed to be hoping I'd just say yes to what he had mumbled so far. Like maybe, on some off chance, I had imagined it with him and he wasn't alone. Jake laughed a little, but it was sad. I could tell he thought something was wrong in his own head. Just a few days ago, it had been me sinking into that hole of doubt. Nothing was worse than thinking you were going crazy.

"There were so many of them."

"What was it, Jake?"

"They were along the ground like they were crawling. Some darted in between the shrubs. I swear I even saw some in the trees. High up in the trees."

"Jake?"

"People, or at least the shadows of people. Dozens of them. Maybe even a hundred. Like the place was being swarmed." He folded his hands, his knuckles white with worry. "I thought we were being attacked or something. But the feeling in my gut wasn't what I'd normally feel if I were going to be in some kind of altercation with a violent perp. Or perps. I mean, I was trained to handle situations like that."

"What did you feel?"

"I felt terrified. The drums kept getting louder in my head, and these black things were shifting and moving in all the shadows. At first I thought they were men. Then they looked like dogs or wolves. In the trees, it was like they transformed into birds. Big birds."

Shape-shifters. A very common American Indian concept.

"Cath, I was so freaked out I drew my weapon."

My breath caught in my throat. That was a last resort for Jake. In Wonder Falls, the need for any of the officers to draw their gun was pretty rare. I wouldn't say it didn't happen, but it was more as a precaution than a real intent to use the weapon. For Jake to admit to this meant he was not only scared of what was out there but scared of his own response to it.

"Right as I was about to start shooting, Blake walked back into the room. He didn't immediately see me out on the balcony. I swung around and had my gun aimed right at him. By the grace of God, I didn't pull the trigger."

Jake's eyes were red. He was doing everything in

his power to not break down and start crying, not that I would have blamed him if he had.

"Do you realize what I could have done, Cath? I could have killed my partner! All because I was hallucinating these things in the courtyard, hearing drums in my head. What the hell?"

"Jake, you need to talk to Bea. Tell her this happened."

"I didn't want to worry her. That's why I came to you. I had to tell someone."

"It's okay, Jake."

"Bea has been picking up on things, hasn't she?" His face was concerned.

"You should really talk to her, Jake. I couldn't say for sure." The last thing I wanted was to get in the middle of their marriage. That would be a no-win situation.

"I'm so amazed by her. I'm amazed by her whole family. Even you. How you guys deal with your gifts I don't know. It was scary at first. But after some of the things I've seen Bea do, I sort of feel, well, unworthy."

This was a very strong contrast to what Blake had said in my room the previous night. He'd seemed very sure that Jake felt the same way he did. "Jake will back me up on this," he had said in that smug, condescending way he always talked to me. Did Blake think just because they were partners Jake would choose him over his family? Did Blake think we would do something so selfish as to make Jake choose? It made no sense, but my blood boiled just the same.

"That is the last thing you should feel around Bea. For whatever reason, she thinks the sun rises and sets on you. But Aunt Astrid did drop her on her head when she was a baby," I teased, nudging Jake with my elbow. He smiled, as I'd hoped he would. "Talk to her. You'll feel better."

He wiped his eyes quickly and stood up, helping me to my feet.

"You're right, Cath."

I smiled up at him and punched him in the arm.

He punched me back, and it throbbed.

"Ouch. You big brute. Police brutality," I mumbled at him, smiling.

Between him and me, this exchange was the equivalent of an *I love you*.

"Here comes Blake. Don't say anything…"

"Oh, gosh no, Jake. I won't. In fact, I've got to get back to my room. It's facials and mud baths today. I'll see you back at home. Talk to Bea."

Coming out of the wooden door marked

MANAGER, Blake had his nose buried in his small leather notebook just as he had when he'd come to my room. Instead of looking down like I normally would have when walking past Blake, I felt I needed to hold my head high. He thought I was weird, crazy, and who knew what else. I was sorry for him. The world held so much mystery, and he was completely closed to it. What a sad existence to never witness a miracle because you chose to keep your eyes closed.

"Oh, uh, Cath, can I—" he started to speak, but I shook my head and quickly walked past him. In my haste, I headed right toward the open elevator, spun around, pressed the number three, let the doors close, and held my breath.

Bracing myself, I listened as the cables clicked and jolted like normal. Within seconds I was on the third floor, my stomach flipping as the elevator car settled and the doors began to open. A burst of adrenaline propelled me out of the car and into the hallway like a stuntman in a J.J. Abrams film, startling an older couple approaching from the direction opposite my room.

"Sorry. Excuse me," I said to their wide-eyed stares. With long strides, I marched down the hallway to my room. I walked around the bed, pulled the balcony curtains open, cracked the door to get in a few breaths of fresh air, snapped on the television, and lay down on the bed to let the rest of my food digest.

I must have dozed off, because before I knew what was happening, I awoke to a wild pounding at my door.

Run

Bea had always been the one of us to keep her cool. In classes at school, when a pop quiz was announced, she'd calmly pull out a pencil. When the roof at the café started to leak after we had had more than a week's worth of rain pour down on us in three days, she placed some buckets and just folded her arms, waiting for the sun to come out.

I, on the other hand, could freak out at the slightest ripple in my regular routine. It wasn't that I didn't like surprise parties or enjoy a good scare at Halloween, but if my car's "check engine" light went on, as it often did, I would fret, lose sleep, chew my nails, and pace the floor until I could get it to the shop for a tune-up.

To see Bea with her long red hair spilling all

around her face, three different pencils sticking out from it, and her lip trembling—well, it scared me more than being stuck in the elevator.

"What?" I said, grabbing her by the hand and pulling her into my room. "Did you find something good? Did something happen to you in the elevator?"

"You're not going to believe what I found out."

"Yeah, you're right, because heaven knows when I'm around you, everything is normal and calm. What? What? Tell me."

"Do you know where Mom is? She wasn't in her room."

I looked at the clock. Aunt Astrid had been gone an hour.

"She went for a walk."

"By herself? Where?"

"Along the grounds. She said she was going to check the path those kids took and see if something was left there."

"We've got to get to her. She might be in serious danger."

Without another word, we both hurried out of my room, down the stairs, and out into the fresh early morning.

"She headed this way." I pointed to a path of

rust-colored mulch that gradually turned into gravel. We hadn't taken this path when I was still carrying the astral spiders as a backpack, so this was unfamiliar to Bea and me.

"Is it just me, or does this path seem a little darker than the one we took the other day?"

Bea nodded.

"I was just thinking that. Is it the branches? Are they thicker?" She looked up, but neither of us said anything more. We looked into the pretty scenery that to both of us had become a little more sinister.

Turning around, I kept checking to see if we were being followed, but I never saw or heard anything.

Sweat started to form on my forehead, and my breath was getting a little shorter. Both Bea and I were practically running, our heads on swivels as we searched in every direction.

"There she is!" Bea yelled, pointing through the trees to a small clearing.

Had anyone been walking past, they might have thought Aunt Astrid was practicing Falun Gong, but we knew different.

"Mom!" Bea shouted as she ran toward Aunt Astrid. I was bringing up the rear, unable to shake the feeling we were being watched by a lot of eyes.

"Mom! Mom!" Aunt Astrid didn't respond, and when we finally got to her, we could see why.

As a witch who could slip easily from one dimension to another, my aunt would sometimes appear to just be staring into space, lost in a daydream. Bea and I had seen her hundreds of times carrying on complete conversations or watching some unseen play unfold in front of her, yet we saw and heard nothing. Shaking her or snapping her out of it was out of the question.

That was what made seeing her like that all the more unnerving.

Her hair was always wild, but now it was charged with static, causing the strands to stand in an unnatural halo around her head. Her hands were gnarled as if she were holding an invisible bar, her shoulders were hunched and rigid, and her arms moved as if she were pulling taffy. But it was her face that made both Bea and me gasp.

My aunt's rosy, round face had been pulled down into an ashy and deeply creviced mask. Her lips had become just things, dark slips that curled and trembled as if she were mumbling a prayer. A thin line of drool dripped down her chin. Her eyes had rolled over to show the whites. They didn't blink, and heaven only knew what she was seeing.

"Do you hear that?" Bea asked, her whisper cutting through the silence of this little clearing like a chainsaw.

I listened but didn't hear anything. Not a thing. Not a bird. Not a cricket. Not a breeze. Nothing. My shoulders shook as I looked around us.

It wasn't a huge figure, maybe the size of a cat or a raccoon. That was what I thought was there when I saw the movement out of the corner of my eye. I turned my head to the left, only to see the trees we had run past to get to Aunt Astrid. The path was right beyond it just a few paces. Never in my life had I wanted to be somewhere so badly. Just on the path. It was a man-made path. The people from the spa took this nature walk. It was real and it went somewhere.

Then something moved to my right. I looked, but nothing was there.

Get ahold of yourself, Cath.

I called out to any animals that might have been in the vicinity, hiding, peeking, wondering what the heck was going on just like we were.

"You're sure you don't hear that?" Bea said, slipping her hand around my arm and pulling me closer to her as she looked nervously around.

"I don't hear a thing. Nothing at all," I said, my

voice shaking. "Bea, what should we do? Should we wake her up?"

"We aren't supposed to. She always said we'd cause more harm than good if we snapped her out of one of her trances, but...she doesn't look right."

I looked at Astrid's face and watched her for a moment.

"Bea, is she breathing?"

Bea's head snapped to her mother, and we both stared. Was her chest rising and falling like it should have been? Were her lips turning blue?

"If this is where those kids died, maybe what got them has got my mom!" Bea cried. She leaned close to her mom and listened. "I don't feel a breath, Cath! What should we do?"

I stared. My mind wouldn't start. It just turned over and over without kicking into gear.

"Cath!" Bea cried. "Mom! Mom!"

If it were my mother, I'd suffer the lecture about leaving her to her own methods if it meant getting her back. With all my strength, I slapped my aunt across the face, screaming at her to wake up.

Her body jerked to the left, and I thought for sure she was going to fall over. But she jerked back up and sneered at me, those white eyes staring me down.

"Give her back!" Bea yelled, grabbing her mother by the shoulders.

Whatever was in there didn't want Bea's hands on it. The repelling force was so strong it threw Bea back about five feet to land with a solid thud on her butt. Aunt Astrid also collapsed in the soft grass where she had been standing.

Bea didn't hesitate.

"Mom?" she kept babbling over and over as she quickly crawled to her mother's side. "Mom? Are you okay?" Tears had soaked her cheeks.

I knelt down and took my aunt's hand. She was panting as if she had been holding her breath for a long time. I watched as the color slowly crept back up into her face and her eyes blinked back to their normal color, as clear and twinkling as ever they had been.

"I'm all right, Bea." She rubbed her daughter's head and wiped the tears from her cheeks. Then she rubbed her own cheek, and I saw her wince.

"I'm sorry, Aunt Astrid. I had to give you a crack. I didn't know what else to do."

"Well, I won't have to worry about you if that Officer Warner gets fresh, I suppose." She stretched her jaw to the right and the left then smiled at me.

"What the heck was that, Mom? You had us

scared to death. You weren't breathing. You weren't moving. Your face was all..."

"Gross," I added, hoping a little levity might help calm Bea down.

"Yeah, gross," Bea said, slowly getting her composure back. We both stood up and reached down to help Aunt Astrid to her feet. Once she was up, she wobbled a little but seemed to be coming back to us completely. Before we could let go of her hands, she clutched us both tightly.

"I'm glad you did that," she said. A sound came from my aunt's mouth that I rarely heard. Not just fear. Terror. "I'm glad you got me out of there."

"Out of where?" I shook my head. "And can we get out of here while we are at it? This whole place is making me jumpy. I'm seeing things and stuff is moving and the birds aren't singing and, well, it's all just a little unnatural."

"Yes. Let's get out of here."

"Can you walk okay, Mom?"

"Honey, I think we better run."

Enisi

It didn't take us long to make it back to the spa. We didn't talk. We just panted our way back up the path we had come down and didn't stop until we had reached the lobby entrance.

"I'm a sweaty mess," I said, pulling at my shirt, which was sticking to my back.

"We've got our facials, mud baths, and hot spring soaks waiting for us. I say we just go relax, get ourselves settled, and talk amongst the living."

"I couldn't agree more," my aunt said. Shrugging, I didn't say a word and followed my family into the spa.

While we were getting into our robes in the women's changing room, my aunt began to talk quietly. We were the only ones in there, but discretion was the word of the day.

"I just thought I'd see what I could see," she began.

Without knowing exactly where she was headed, Aunt Astrid had let the guides of the other plane take over and lead her in the right direction. Channeling those spirits was something she was used to doing. It had never scared her before, nor had she ever had a spirit consume her so she'd have a problem getting back to this dimension. But the land around the Muskox was not like the rest of Wonder Falls.

"It is like Grand Central Station," she said as a petite woman of Asian descent slathered my cheeks with dark-gray, almost black clay. "There are spirits coming and going from all directions, and not all of them are what we'd normally see," she said, looking at me.

"Oh man. You mean more spiders." I shook my head and wrinkled my nose. "What the heck? Who do you get to exterminate those things for good?"

The little woman who was rubbing my face finished and laid two cucumber slices on my eyes. They were ice cold and felt fantastic. Each of us was stretched out on her own white table as soothing music played and a small water fountain bubbled happily in the background. A half dozen candles burned, giving off the scent of lemongrass.

Aunt Astrid peeked from under her cucumbers and saw we were finally alone in the room.

"I didn't want to say too much in mixed company. So let me be quick. The Muskox Serenity Spa and Retreat Center is a beacon for any spirit from any dimension to pass into this one."

"That makes sense," Bea said. "I discovered a few things on the Internet about this place and what is going on that probably has the multidimensional door standing wide open."

"And I've decided you two witches are not taking me on any more vacations ever." I took a deep breath of the lemongrass-scented air.

Aunt Astrid went first.

Her journey into the alternative dimension had not been just chance. Her guide had told her he was waiting for her and that she had to speak with their Enisi.

"I couldn't get a fix on my guide. He was strong, but he kept changing, altering his appearance so he just seemed like a shadow."

"Was he a shadow person? Aren't those trouble all on their own?" My face was starting to tighten, and I felt the cool mud drying when I tapped it with my fingertips.

"No. Not a shadow person like the kind they claim to see on all those ghost-hunter shows. And not a person who is still alive but his essence, his supernatural fingerprint, is showing up like in room 116. No. I believe this was a shape-shifter."

I remembered what Jake had said and swallowed hard.

"Before I started to follow him, I looked around me. Of course, I wasn't seeing the landscape that you girls found me in. I saw the blurry outline of the spa in the distance, the path I had walked on, but spirits were everywhere. They were not necessarily in the dimension I had slipped into. But this place, this land had brought them there. Some looked as if they were studying the place, maybe searching for someone that looked familiar. Others gave off a more insidious aura. Like if the opportunity to trip an old woman or prick a child with a pin came up, they might take it. And still others hid in shadows, seething with red-hot eyes.

"Finally our journey started. I walked for miles and probably didn't even take a step in this world. Isn't it funny?" Aunt Astrid mused for a moment. "This shape-shifting guide took me through fields of tall grass, over a small brook of perfectly clear water, and up a hill. Once at the top, he became very nervous. He told me to stand where I was, and I wondered where in the world he thought I would go."

"Weren't you scared?" I asked. "Neither one of us was there. I think we might have to have a long talk about stranger danger and going off with shape-shifters when we get home, right Bea?"

"Oh, yes, we are going to have a long talk about this kind of reckless behavior when we get back to Wonder Falls."

"I wasn't scared. Not at first. I could smell clean, fresh air. Air like I've never smelled before. Honey-suckle bloomed far off in the distance, and I swear I could smell it from where I was standing. I looked around, turning in a circle, but before I noticed my guide had disappeared, the sky clouded over with dark, low-lying clouds."

I propped myself up on my elbow and took the cucumbers off my eyes. Bea had the same thought.

"Then the Enisi showed up." I watched my aunt's face become pale. She chewed at her lip for a few minutes as if she was thinking that maybe she shouldn't say anything. Her throat extended for a second as she swallowed hard.

"She couldn't have been more than four feet tall. Skinny wasn't the word for her. She was bony, and her joints stuck out like knots on a tree. Her skin was the same color and texture, like she had spent her entire life working under a bright, hot sun. Very little hair grew on her head, but scant gray and wiry strands stood out randomly in brittle tufts over her scalp."

I looked at Bea, who stared at her mother with her mouth open.

"When she spoke, I could see her purplish lips moving. She had about four teeth in her mouth, and they were mostly black. But her eyes were the most unsettling. Something lurked behind them. At first I thought they were white with cataracts. But she got in my face, right up to my face, and glared at me with those eyes. Something was in them."

"What do you mean something was in them?" Bea asked, her lips barely moving as our masks tightened.

"Something was moving in them. Spirits. Ghosts. Souls. And what I heard her say terrified me." Aunt Astrid had been lying on her back with her hands nervously picking at the top of the robe she was wrapped in. Taking the cucumbers off her eyes, she smiled nervously at us.

"Mom, would you like some water?" Bea swung her legs over the side of the table she had been lying on.

"Actually, I could use something a good bit stronger." She reached over and patted Bea's knee.

"What did she say to you, Aunt Astrid?"

"Well, the language she was speaking, the words coming out of her mouth, I didn't understand. But I heard a voice in my ears. It was that voice inside me that was scary." Aunt Astrid's eyes focused on a spot in front of her as if everything else were too bright. "In my head I could hear it. It was raspy and child-like at the same time, sending a needle of terror down into my stomach. And if this Enisi was old, her voice sounded even older, if that makes any sense. She said it wouldn't stop."

"That what wouldn't stop?" I heard the question come out of my mouth, but I was pretty sure I knew what the answer was going to be.

"The deaths."

Hot Spring

Yup. I was right.

"She said that she would continue to collect those souls as long as she was summoned, and she would never stop being summoned. Then she started to laugh and pointed a long, bony finger off to a high cliff behind us. A figure stood there. He was in a pitch-black shadow from a brilliant sunset behind him. I couldn't see his eyes, but I felt them."

"Then the Enisi took hold of my arm. Her old, gnarly hands were like eagle talons, and they squeezed hard until I thought I was going to scream. She started to laugh at me, pointing to other creatures and people drifting around like she was letting them all know I was there and I wasn't like them. I wasn't. I was alive. But she cackled at me as I tried to pull away from her, and that was when you guys got me out of there."

I watched my aunt take a deep breath, still rubbing her hands together and worrying a hangnail on her thumb.

"Even though I am back here in my dimension, I can see some of those things that I saw there. They are looking for me. Maybe they hope I can bring them back here. Or maybe they want to feed here. I don't know for sure. But I'm afraid the longer I am in this place, the more dangerous it is going to get for all of us."

We all sat in silence until the curtain separating our quiet room from the hallway was pushed aside and my Asian facial technician entered with her two companions.

Both Aunt Astrid and Bea jumped and let out yelps of surprise just as I did. I clutched my heart and let out a relieved chuckle.

Without another word, we were each swiveled over to our own big bowls of cool rose water, and our faces were gently and thoroughly washed clean.

The women explained to us that now that our faces were detoxified, we were ready to have the rest of our bodies as thoroughly cleansed in the mud bath. I wasn't really listening to her speech on where the mud was from, what kind of kelp or seaweed was mixed with it, and how the water from the hot springs kept it at a constant ninety degrees. I thought that sounded kind of hot, but since I was only half listening, I didn't give it too much thought.

The three of us stepped into a dimly candlelit room. It was a very romantic setting, and out of nowhere a thought of Officer Tom Warner popped into my head.

He should have been the last thing on my mind. My aunt had been telling us about her traumatic experience with an old hag. This was no time for romance.

"Okay, who's first?" the spa technician asked happily.

After a few moments of hesitation, each one of us slowly but surely sank up to our necks in the charcoal-colored goo. It was a little unnerving at first, and I didn't like the idea of not being able to see what was in there with me.

Of course, there was nothing in the mud but minerals and dirt and seaweed and me. That was all. Still, I didn't really like how it felt and would probably be hopping out sooner rather than later.

"Okay, Mom. You need to hang on to your hat,

because I found out stuff, too. But you tell me if you think it fits together."

Bea seemed to be so wrapped up in her part of the story that I don't even think she realized she was sitting in mud. To her this was just a very fluid, dark blanket that was keeping her warm and pulling the impurities out of her body. To me it was a soupy mess. But I calmed myself down, leaned back against the hard, curved basin that was designed to look like rock, and listened to what Bea had to say. She hadn't even begun to explain to me anything she had found out before we had gone off in search of her mom.

"So, with just a few slight variations on the story Maureen the waitress told us about the teenagers that died, the *legend* of the cursed land was pretty much spot on."

It was a little freaky for me to look at Bea across the wide tub filled with mud, because she looked like she was just a talking head.

"But a few missing details make this story a little more coherent but a little more sinister, too.

"According to the folklore of unincorporated Wonder Falls, a Chief Big Running Fox and his people did roam along this territory. Some kind of exchange occurred that was not beneficial to his people, the exact details being lost or hazy at best.

"When the chief found out he had been swindled, he did put a curse on the land. Now it isn't clear if he kidnapped two people who happened to be siblings or if he chose them on purpose." Bea tried to use her hands, but the mud made it nearly impossible to move. "But I read a tiny blurb that said the chief poisoned these two people as an offering to Nanbohzo, their god of vengeance. Now, you'd think it would have stopped there after the sacrifice, but no such luck."

It was as if Bea had known this information all her life and had just been waiting for the right moment to bring it up. She could remember facts and figures like she was reciting a grocery list.

"Whether the chief was aware of this or not, and I think he was, Mars was in a superior conjunction with Earth. Venus was at its eastern elongation, and we had a crescent moon. This all happens like clockwork every six years."

She stopped talking and looked at us as if we were supposed to be on the same page as her.

"And…" Aunt Astrid shrugged, getting mud on her cheeks.

"These spirits are still here," Bea said sadly. "Every six years, they reenact the sacrifice. Not to mention the placement of the moon lights the place up like a beacon *and* leaves the doors to several astral planes open for other entities to come and go as they please, as it will stay open for several days. Once it is shut, any wayward spirits are stuck here. But in six years, another set of people will be sacrificed and the door will be left open, and the revenge will continue."

"So what do we have to do to fix this?" I was hoping the time was almost up for the mud bath. This was not my idea of feeling good. I didn't care how clean it made my pores.

"We have to tell the chief his land is safe. That he can move on now," Bea said. Her eyes were sad, and I could tell this bothered her. It wasn't like the usual spirits or bug-a-boos we dealt with. This was a proud leader who had been done wrong not only by the new settlers but by his own kind. He had to be suffering unspeakable heartbreak.

"Why do I get the feeling that this has to be done sooner rather than later, and it is going to have to be done by a couple of people, oh, who could they be... maybe us?" I scratched my head and got mud in my hair.

"And Mom, I hate to say this, but it is your area of expertise. Do you feel up to it?"

My aunt nodded.

We sat there in silence for a couple of minutes. Bea looked as if she was solving some mathematical equation in her head, and my aunt, well, as always, was probably watching the comings and goings of the closest dimension. I felt like I was sitting in glue and couldn't take it anymore.

"I'm done here, guys. I don't like this." I began my slow ascent from what looked like the primordial soup.

"Jeez, I thought it was just me," my aunt said, standing up.

"I'm with you guys," Bea said, rising and helping her mother as well.

We all got out, stood on the smooth, pebbled area of the room that was underneath the showers, and began to wipe ourselves off.

"This feels better than the mud." I got nods of approval from my family.

"I am looking forward to the hot springs, though," Aunt Astrid said.

"Me, too. And I also heard that the Indians of the area used to sit in those sometimes before they sat in their sweat lodges."

"What in the world is a sweat lodge?"

"Native American men would sit in those when they needed answers, needed to resolve a conflict, or

maybe before a battle or hunt. It was a small struc-
ture where they heated some rocks, poured water on
them to get steam, and then sat there." My aunt's
eyes twinkled.

"And then what?" I asked.

"And then they waited for their visions."

"Okay. Well, maybe you'll have a vision that will
help you with our task at hand. It doesn't sound too
bad. I mean, you're just telling this chief he can cross
over. You've helped spirits do that before. This
shouldn't be too hard, right?"

"I'm not sure. There is the Enisi to deal with."

"What do you mean, Mom?"

"Well, I'm sure Chief Big Running Fox is tired.
Every time this lunar formation takes place, he must
mount his horse and come back to the site of so
much pain. I don't believe he likes it. But I didn't get
that feeling from the Enisi."

Bea and I stopped and looked at Aunt Astrid as
the water washed away the mud from our skin in a
cool, refreshing spray. It was a complete contradic-
tion to the hot fear that had started to grow in my
stomach.

"The Enisi was his counselor. She was his muse
and confidant. She had his ear at every turn and,
well, this might be one of those instances where she

is more interested in getting him to continue his revenge because it is somehow helping her, feeding her. I believe she is getting stronger each time that lunar thingamajig takes place."

"Can't you get her to cross over, too?"

"Well, I can try."

"Ladies?" came the voice of our spa technician and her entourage. "Why are you out of the mud bath so soon? You still have ten minutes." She seemed shocked at our rebellious behavior.

"It wasn't for us," Bea said tactfully. "We're ready for our soak in the hot springs."

"Well, it won't be ready for ten more minutes. You can wait in the lounge area. There is ice water to drink or orange juice if you prefer." She gave us a quick smile and held the curtain back for us to exit the mud bath room.

We sat down around a small table and each enjoyed a glass of ice water with cucumbers in it.

"And the thing about this Enisi," Aunt Astrid continued, "she is cruel. Cruel for sport. I can feel it."

I didn't like the sound of this.

We sat there, and I let Aunt Astrid's words sink in. I thought about all the evil that surrounded me. This was supposed to be a relaxing getaway, and all this chaos—murders, astral spiders, evil spirits—was so absurd that I wanted to laugh.

After a while, our friend the spa technician came into the waiting room.

"Okay ladies. If you'll follow me."

She led us down a long corridor to an open patio. The air was heavy and thick with moisture like a greenhouse might be. We followed her down a cedar-planked path that gave way to more smooth stones and a lovely, crystal-clear pool of water. Steam rose from the water and wove and curled its way through the air in delicate plumes.

We each removed our robes and climbed in. All at once we let out a collective "ahhh."

"Now this is nice," Bea said, leaning her head back and closing her eyes.

I watched my aunt, who gave me a wink and rolled her head to the left and right.

The water was hot. I nestled onto a shelf of stone, let my legs float, and inched myself down until the water was just below my chin. I could hear the birds and the flitter of leaves from behind us over the cedar wall that blocked off the elements of nature for just a little privacy. The steam continued to rise, and I felt all the tension and nervousness leaving my shoulders and my back.

As the birds chirped and squawked, I called out to them.

"Hey, how's everyone doing out there?" My mind was feeling soft and loose.

"Good. Not bad. Too many squirrels." Then I heard a great squawking among all of them as they all agreed on too many squirrels. *"Eating our sunflower seeds. Always the sunflowers. Stealing the sunflower seeds."*

"I'll see if I can't get more seeds out there for you." I smiled a little as I watched through slit eyes the steam becoming thicker until finally it seemed like I was the only one in the water. I wasn't scared. In fact, I was so relaxed that I stretched my arms and legs out and didn't feel the sides of the spring. It felt like I was floating on the water, which rippled gently beneath me, carrying me off to another place, maybe even another time; I couldn't tell. I didn't want to open my eyes. I just wanted to drift in the hot water.

The sounds of the birds got farther and farther away. It wasn't long before all I could hear was the water lapping over itself. I found no rocks to sit on anymore, no shore. It was just one vast body of water with me as a speck in the middle of it.

But that isn't where I am, I thought to myself. *I'm in a small hot spring. My aunt and cousin are just within arm's reach.* I stretched out but felt nothing.

With all the courage I could muster, I pointed my toe down and lowered my leg. Any minute now, any second, it would brush against the stone bottom. It had to be there. But I felt nothing. In a great panic, I pulled my legs up and snapped my eyes open.

Finally I found the bottom. In fact, I could stand up in the little pool, and the water would just be below my nose. It wasn't deep at all.

I was in complete darkness except for the crescent moon staring down at me, reflecting off the ripples of water. What had happened? How had I gotten out here?

"Help!" My voice echoed off of nothing. "Help! Bea! Aunt Astrid!"

My heart drummed in my ears.

I spun around in the water, looking behind me for anything to grab on to. Then I realized it wasn't my heart making that noise. It was actual drums. Like Indian drums. Like they were getting ready for battle.

I tried to scream again, but water filled my mouth. Something had pulled me under for just a second, letting me up almost instantly. I gasped and choked. Again came a tug on my foot, and my head dipped beneath the surface, only to pop back up. I tried to call out, but nothing but coughs and chokes came out of my mouth.

Then, as if in slow motion, I felt one finger at a time wrap around my ankle tightly. I tried to pull my leg away, but where was I going to go? It could see me, but I couldn't see it. It held me fast. Kicking did no good. With a grip that felt like it was going to sever my foot from my ankle, I was yanked under the surface of the water, and this time it kept me there.

I opened my eyes in the black water and saw the hot-red eyes staring at me from the distorted face of the old crone I could only assume was the Enisi. She screamed at me, her mouth long and horrifying and ready to swallow me up.

But before I gulped up half the water around me, I saw another face. It was Bea!

Evil Old Biddy

Bea was in the water too. Her face was determined and...angry. She grabbed hold of the Enisi. In a huge flash of light, I snapped my eyes open, sat bolt upright, and took a huge, loud gulp of air.

"Oh, Cath!" I heard Aunt Astrid calling to me. "Get her on her side. Pat her on the back. There you go, sweetheart. Just cough it out. You're okay now."

I felt like a prize poodle on display. Dozens of eyes followed me as I coughed and gagged, and the look on the poor spa technician's face sent me to tears.

Looking at Bea, who herself was out of breath, I could see she knew. We had been together in that other place. If it hadn't been for her, I thought I very well might be visiting Davy Jones's locker right about then.

"I'm all right," I managed to gurgle. "I'm okay." Taking a couple of deep breaths and shaking my head, I sat up. Aunt Astrid put a robe around me. My foot was hanging over the edge of the small pool of water in which I had been relaxing just minutes ago. It took a nanosecond for me to pull my foot away from the edge.

"We'll call you an ambulance," the technician said, worried by not just my condition but whatever trouble she thought she might be in.

"No." I put my hand up quickly. "No. No ambulance. It's my fault. I have allergies. I took an antihistamine. Bad idea. No. I don't need an ambulance. Really."

It was a lie. This pool of water was part of the curse. All three of us were targets, and a trip to the hospital would just delay our helping the poor Indian chief get his well-deserved rest and perhaps sending this Enisi off to…somewhere else.

"Really, I'm all right."

"We'll take her back to her room. She'll be better after a rest." Aunt Astrid and Bea helped me to my feet. I stood for a moment. Nothing tilted or whirled around my head, and one step was easily followed by another.

I will admit the idea of getting out of my bathing suit and into some comfy clothes and away from the water and the mud and all the rubberneckers sounded ideal.

We got through the lobby and piled into the elevator, where I had to let out a sigh.

"I never thought I'd be this scared of anything, but I'll be honest and tell you guys if I never set foot in an elevator or pool of water again, it will be too soon. I don't even think I can take a bath ever again. How about you, Bea?"

"That is one evil old biddy we are going to be dealing with. Her magic is as old as ours," Bea said angrily.

"Are you all right, Bea?" I slipped my hand into hers.

"When I touched her, I saw what she was made up of. Aunt Astrid is right. She's evil and likes it. She's the one who takes the beauty of nature and twists it into ugliness. She makes it scary."

"Like the chipmunks!" I shouted as the elevator stopped and bobbed before the doors opened.

"Chipmunks?" my aunt asked.

I told them about the chipmunks I had seen while

I was still under assault by the astral spiders and how depressed that image had made me.

"That sounds about right," Bea said. "She's had her eye on us since we arrived, I think."

Once we were all in my room, we sat quietly for a few moments. I was on one bed. Aunt Astrid was on the other. Bea sat at the desk.

"So. What is the plan?" I looked at both of them.

"We need to get ready. I'll go to my room and get my bag."

"What bag, Mom?"

"My witch's bag. Never leave home without it."

She stepped outside, leaving Bea and me alone. Suddenly I remembered what Jake had told me. He'd asked me not to tell Bea. He didn't want her to worry. But something inside me said I had to. I wouldn't tell her everything. I'd let him fill in the gory details. But I should say something.

"I saw Jake this morning," I said. Bea smiled at the mention of his name.

"Yeah, poor guy was up all night."

"He told me that something happened that scared him."

"He did?"

I gave her a Reader's Digest version of what he'd said. I left out a lot, including the gun.

"He could probably use a shoulder to lean on."

"My poor guy," Bea said. "He puts up with so much, and I sometimes wonder if he'd have any of these problems if I wasn't... you know, the way I am."

"If you guys aren't just the most sickeningly sweet couple I've ever seen. Good heavens." I smirked, rolling my eyes. "First of all, Jake would run into a burning building for you. Second, you'd do the same for him. That kind of love is what the world needs. Not the safe kind that stays while times are good or each person is healthy and normal. Real love thrives on the weirdness, the oddities, the strange little ticks and twitches that make people different."

"And how would you know about this, Miss Cath? That sounds like the poetry of a woman in the throes of passion." Bea began to fan herself with her hand. "Don't tell me that handsome Officer Tom Warner has moved you to spouting sonnets."

I rolled my eyes but felt my cheeks blush, and when I heard Bea start to laugh, I knew she had seen them turn red too.

"He seems nice" was all I said.

"Yes, he does, and he seems very interested in you. But..."

"But what?"

Bea stood up and sat across from me on the other bed.

"I just always thought I saw something between you and Blake. Even though you guys fight and bicker and all that."

"What are you talking about? He's dating Darla."

"Oh, come on! Do you really think that is going to last? And are they really dating, or are they just sort of hanging out together? It isn't like she doesn't have a reputation around town."

"Oh, yeah, guys *never* want to be with girls who have *reputations*." Did I mention how much I loved to use sarcasm?

Bea was used to it and started to laugh. I changed into an oversized T-shirt and leggings.

"Besides, maybe I don't want to be with a guy who's gone out with Darla Castellan."

I didn't dare say anything about what Blake had said to me about my family. A pang of anger plucked at my heart just thinking about him sitting where Bea had been a few seconds ago, telling me how crazy I was, how nothing had happened at the Prestwick house and how even Jake felt that way. No. I'd keep that to myself.

"Hey, it's your life. I certainly wouldn't discourage you from going out with Tom Warner.

Are you going to call him when we get back home?"

"*If* we get back home? Maybe."

Bea nodded and smiled a little. "There is always a chance things could go south. But I don't think it will be this time."

"What makes you so sure?"

Bea didn't say anything more but just shrugged.

We were startled by the knock that came from the door. With Bea there, I wasn't scared and opened it for my Aunt Astrid, now wearing one of her long hippy dresses, who bustled inside holding a green carpetbag that was packed so full I could have sworn I heard the seams crying out.

"Okay, girls. Let's get started."

Okima

✤

All of us could tell things were going to be difficult. We had no references, no real supplies, no way of knowing what we were really dealing with. I felt like MacGyver trying to make a bomb out of two paperclips, an inch of duct tape, and a piece of chewing gum.

But I had learned my lesson from the Prestwick house. No way was I going to rush anything, second-guess my aunt's instructions, or let my emotions get in the way. We had to be one united front if we were going to be of any help at all.

While Bea did a cleansing of us and the room, I looked out onto the balcony. The sun had set about fifteen minutes previously. The beautiful landscape had become menacing as the bare branches stood darker against the sky, and shadows covered almost every square inch of the grounds. Even the little lights around the paths seemed to have grown dimmer, as if their batteries were low.

Normally, Aunt Astrid would call to the guardians of the surrounding dimensions to come to our aid if we began to falter. However, although she tried to shoot up a psychic flare to get their attention, it was not generating the response she had hoped.

"This place is being cloaked or something," she said. "I can't seem to get anyone out there to notice us."

"Perhaps it's too noisy. Like you said, this whole area has become a terminal for wayward spirits. Have you ever tried to get someone's attention at an airport? Or at the train station, especially when it's rush hour? You need an air horn, police lights, and a megaphone." Bea shrugged.

"It might not be the greatest idea to let the guardians know we are in need of help. Just because you call them doesn't mean they are the ones who will answer, right?" Here I was, the eternal optimist, always looking on the bright side of every situation.

"You're right. There is just *too* much activity. I didn't even think of that." Aunt Astrid slapped her hand against her head. "You're both right. We'll have to see what happens, and if we get in trouble, well, we'll just have to rely on each other."

"I'd rather rely on you guys than anyone else in the world," I said, pulling my hair back from my face. "Besides, this doesn't sound like a tough job. You're just helping this Indian chief cross over to the light, right? That shouldn't be so hard."

"You're forgetting the Enisi," Aunt Astrid said. "If he listens to her in death like he did in life, we may be in for a bigger fight than we are prepared for. Normally I'd have my books. I know back at my house I have some things on the Native American holy men. I remember a simple ritual of thanks. But right now the best I have is Wikipedia, and that doesn't ease my mind."

With the room filled with sage smoke (and the smoke detector batteries removed—thank goodness the detectors weren't hardwired), our minds and bodies clear, and the energy in and around us unblocked, we made our simple plan and headed toward the clearing in which Bea and I had stumbled on Aunt Astrid that afternoon.

It was much slower going in the darkness. The crescent moon was easily seen in the sky but gave off little light.

"I'm sorry, guys, but darkness hasn't been my

friend these last few days," I whispered. "Is it just me, or is everything getting harder to see? Just please don't let me fall into a body of water."

I felt Bea's hand slip into mine and squeezed it. Her touch was a healing one, and I began to feel the courage she had transferred to me. Aunt Astrid walked ahead of us, her bag still full of things Bea and I knew better than to question.

"I've come to see Okima by the flight of the crow. Let me pass," she murmured over and over in a respectful voice. It was a quiet song that Aunt Astrid kept up. From the sound of her voice, she was not completely with us anymore. She was making her way to the dimension that she had been in earlier that day, the one with the tall grass and the bubbling brook. I wondered how beautiful it must have been in the nighttime, too, when the land was wild.

Bea and I didn't speak. If Aunt Astrid was crossing over, we just had to follow her for now. So far, I was enjoying this journey. All my aunt had to do was talk with the chief. *How hard could that be, right? Right.* I sounded confident in my head until I heard my aunt's voice begin getting louder and louder.

"I've come to see Okima! By the flight of the crow! Let me pass!" She called out the words, then yelled them, then shouted them, and finally she was screaming at the top of her lungs.

She was hollering so loud that I was sure armed guards or at least the lights from on top of a police car would soon be seen from where we were, officers with weapons drawn running to rescue the senile old lady lost twenty feet from the door she'd left by. But nothing happened. I heard only the sound of crickets and loons, but just as I noticed them, they stopped.

Aunt Astrid began to make her way quickly off the path and to the same clearing she had been in when Bea and I had found her under the influence of the Enisi.

"Should we follow?" I whispered.

Bea's eyes darted around. "I don't know for sure. I'm really not sure what to do."

Pointing off to the right, I saw what Jake had seen the night before: something so unnatural, so unnerving that no breath came out of my mouth.

They were like an army. Shadows separate from any stationary object appeared to be climbing up trees, crawling around the ground, hopping and dancing on the path between Aunt Astrid and us.

They were blacker than the darkness around us and much bigger as they shifted and morphed into different things. I saw a wolf bound over the brush before turning into a sleek cat and running off. A bird with immense wings circled over us before bounding across a small ditch like a deer might. And then I saw the human shapes. They were bulky, menacing things that marched up to us then disappeared. They seemed not to believe we were there and needed a closer look, but before they got to us, the dream ended.

I also noticed oddities. As I looked to my right, I saw what could only be a sasquatch. As my eyes scanned the crowd, I was sure I saw a couple of them. Maybe more. Wolves walking on two legs? Giant spider things? Yet none of them stayed in that form. They dissolved into other things until I wasn't sure if I was seeing anything correctly.

"Bea, are you seeing this, too?" I was always so sure I was hallucinating. My voice was barely audible, but Bea nodded.

The unnerving sight was compounded by the lack of sounds. All we could hear was my aunt repeating her mantra over and over again as she made her way to whatever checkpoint she was looking for on that side of reality. Then the sound of drums shattered the silence. They were slow and steady, crashing in our ears. I saw nothing that looked like anyone playing them, but the shadow figures, the shape-shifters, were becoming more and more obstructive. They were in front of us more than anything, and both Bea and I were struggling to keep an eye on Aunt Astrid.

We could hear her still repeating the chant.

"I've come to see Okima by the flight of the crow. Let me pass."

But we could no longer see her.

White-Skinned Witch

In a bright burst of light, a magnificent fire burst into life in front of all three of us. The flames reached fifteen, maybe twenty feet high, licking and curling in the air. Sparks shot from the dried logs, and I swore I could smell smoke and feel the heat as we drew closer.

That was when the shadows transformed. They were no longer wolves and birds and deer. Instead I saw men with sinewy muscles who glared at us with bottomless eyes. They wore hides and paint on their faces, yet they were not like the pictures drawn in the books I'd read in school as a kid. They were wild, and our rules didn't apply to them. Even in death, they were untamable.

On the other side of the fire I could see women, too. Their long, dark hair hung around their faces.

They wore hides as well. Necklaces with many strands hung around their necks, and they had even more intimidating stares than the men. Some had children at their sides or strapped to their backs.

Leaning over, I was about to say something to Bea, but she had been separated from me. Men who had some feathers in their hair and some beads around their necks had slipped between us unnoticed. They began to sing and chant, too. But it was something other than what my aunt was saying. I had never heard the words before, but in my head I knew what they meant. In a nutshell, we were not welcome.

I thought to push myself through the crowd but changed my mind. This wasn't my place. I was the intruder. I was the one who didn't belong, and I was going to remain respectful until the situation called for something different. I could hear Aunt Astrid but couldn't see her.

With cautious steps I continued to move closer to the fire. Behind the flames, I could just make out the tips of feathers on a massive headdress. A man sat there on what looked like a pile of pelts. I could see his leg and part of an elbow. But I could not see his face. Something told me I didn't want to. Not yet. But curiosity pulled me even closer until I thought I might take hold of one of the man's hands and ask who it was behind the fire.

Would they understand me? Would they answer me? Would they chuck me into the fire that, illusion or not, was brighter than the sun on this exceptionally dark night?

Everything stopped. Immediately, I assumed they had read my thoughts and I was done for. Holding my breath, I watched. The shadows as well as the people parted, leaving Aunt Astrid, Bea, and me the only ones close to the fire. My eyes strained to see what was still moving behind the lines of Natives, but I couldn't get a lock on anything. Instead, I could just see the people scowling at us.

Then, like a crab crawling up on the shore, came what I could only assume was the Enisi. If she weighed eighty pounds, she weighed a lot. Her skin was dark, but I could see in the light of the fire that as bony as she was, she was unnaturally strong.

The drums had stopped, and the only movement was the Enisi coming up to Aunt Astrid. Once in front of her, she slowly stood. Her bent body still cast a shadow from the fire that seemed to engulf my aunt completely.

She spoke in hisses and barks. Again, it was just

my guess, but the mystical translator of the afterlife helped me piece together what she was saying.

"White-skinned witch!" Her words were full of hatred. "He will not hear you!"

"Step aside, Enisi," Aunt Astrid said firmly. "I will speak to your chief."

"He will not hear you!" The old woman squawked like a wounded starling. Her words became jumbled, and before my aunt could move, three giant gray wolves walked out of the crowd and stood before her, teeth bared and hackles raised.

"Your battle is over!" my aunt cried with her hands raised in surrender. "You can go home! Home!"

The Enisi began to laugh. Her mouth was wide open, and her eyes rolled over to show the whites. She didn't want to go home. I couldn't understand why not.

"Home!" she mocked. "This is home! We live in this chaos!" Her white eyes seemed to bore into my aunt. "You have no power here!" The Enisi waved her hand, and the wolves advanced. One snapped at Aunt Astrid's leg, making her shake and stumble backward.

The old crone laughed sadistically. I watched the faces of the people around her, and they looked unsure—unsure that the right thing was being done and unsure that they wanted to stay in this place. Tired was how they looked, yet too scared to speak up.

Another of the wolves advanced on Aunt Astrid, baring its sharp teeth and crouching low. Couldn't anyone stop this? What would happen to us if we were torn apart by shape-shifters in another plane of reality? Would someone find our shredded remains in our reality? Would it just be chalked up to a bizarre animal attack?

"We want to help!" Bea shouted. "Please! Let us help you!"

The Enisi screamed out words I didn't understand, but before I could move, I saw Bea being grabbed and thrown to the ground. Within an instant, one of the wolves bounded with great, terrifying grace around my aunt and towered over Bea, its snout trembling with rage as it revealed its fangs. The creature's golden eyes sparkled in the light from the fire.

"*NO!*" I cried in my head.

The wolf instantly looked up at me, its teeth no longer bared.

"*She doesn't want to hurt you! None of us do! We want to help!*"

The Enisi couldn't hear me. She didn't know I was talking to the wolves.

"We know you've come here to punish the people that took your land. You don't have to anymore. They are all gone. Now it is just innocent people who love your land. No one is going to change it. I know it must've been difficult to see so much suffering, but time can heal, and you can be at peace now."

Slowly and carefully, Bea touched the wolf, and he transformed before our eyes into a young Native American male. His face was stony, but his eyes glowed like those of the animal that he shared his existence with. He spoke in a language I didn't understand, and the other wolves looked at him.

They yapped and barked, snarling and growling, patting the ground in front of them as if trying to make a point.

The young man turned to Bea and said something to her that I know she didn't understand. He looked at me again.

"Can you still hear me?" I asked him.

He didn't speak but nodded slowly.

"Please. Let my cousin talk to your Chief Big Running Fox. Please?"

The man spoke to the Enisi.

Whatever he said made her furious. She began to

scream and wail, her bony arms flailing in all directions, and I noticed a collective step back from
everyone around the fire. What was her story? Why
was she like this? Bea could find out. If she could
just touch the old woman, she might be able to find
something out that could help us.

As of right now, the chief, who I still couldn't see,
was still sitting behind the fire, watching everything
going on. What was he waiting for? Was he in charge
or was this crazy old lady?

I cleared my throat to get Bea's attention. Of
course, it got just about everyone else's attention,
too. Subtle, I knew. But she looked at me. I grabbed
my own wrist and pointed at Bea and then the old
witch as she hopped around screaming and yelling.

Bea nodded. She got up, dusted herself off, and
walked boldly up to her mother's side.

"Bea! Get back!" Aunt Astrid sizzled. "Are
you crazy?"

The crone stopped and glared at her through
milky eyes.

"This woman isn't going to let you pass. I need to
find out why." Without waiting for permission, Bea
walked up to the Enisi and grabbed her wrist.

Within seconds, Bea was screaming and crying
while the old enchantress laughed. Clutching Bea's

hand, she held her fast as Bea tried to pull away, shaking her head and scratching at the bony talon.

"You like what you see, red-headed devil!" the old woman cried.

The wolves that had not transformed back into people were trained on my aunt. The one that had become a man stood aside as if he no longer had a part in any of this. What was going on? Why was this woman so powerful over everyone?

With trembling legs and pounding heart, I ran around the fire and threw myself in front of the chief. I grabbed at his legs and boots, but my hands closed on nothing! The clothes were empty! I looked up and saw the headdress was perched on a wooden stake.

Where was he? Where was his wife, the daughter of the rival tribe? I was seething with anger and whirled around to face the Enisi. She threw Bea back to the ground. My poor cousin collapsed and sobbed, but she was able to speak.

"She's insane, Cath! She's killed so many of them! Her own people and others! Children! She's killed children!"

Gone

❧❧❧

Quickly I spoke to the wolves. They were my only hope. I had to get through to them. Looking into the sky, I saw the glow of an approaching sunrise. My gosh! How long had we been at this? If we didn't get this settled before the sun came up, they'd kill again in another six years.

Where is your chief? Please tell me. I need to speak to him.

One wolf with a diamond-shaped patch of pale-gray fur on his forehead between his eyes howled, yapped, and snapped at me, his teeth still showing in a menacing grin. The other wolf, which had a broader chest and looked like it was older, also snapped at the air and barked, licking its lips hungrily.

She keeps him in the fire. He is always in the fire.

"Keeps him in the fire? What does that mean?" I whined out loud. But whatever I said was enough to knock the grimace off the Enisi's face.

"Aunt Astrid. They said she keeps him in the fire. The chief is in the fire. Do you know what that means?"

With wild eyes, my aunt turned to face the blaze.

"I think I do! I think it means she's keeping him in the dark—misinformed! Misled!"

She pulled a pamphlet from the bag that was still strapped across her body. I squinted to see what it said. It turned out to be the Muskox Spa pamphlet. Tearing it into pieces, my aunt tossed it into the fire then took a step back. It made a tiny burst as the flames turned it into a brown, curling mess before consuming it entirely. She must've been trying to show the chief how the land had changed.

The wolves began to whine. The Enisi screamed and tried to retreat to a dark corner, scurrying along the ground like a...well, I was tired of thinking it, but like a spider.

Suddenly the fire billowed outward. I was afraid for my aunt and ran toward her, grabbing her by the arm and pulling her to the ground beside Bea, who was still trembling from whatever madness she had seen inside the Enisi.

Before I could say anything, a breathtaking horse emerged from the flames. Sitting astride him was a fierce-looking man. His hair, completely gray, hung down in braids, and he wore an even more impressive headdress than the empty one sitting atop the stake behind us.

The Enisi ran to the chief, her mouth moving in words we couldn't understand. Quickly my aunt got to her feet and, holding her hands up, bowed to the chief. From out of the flames stepped a young woman. She was as beautiful as any picture I had ever seen. Her jet-black hair hung well past her waist, and her face looked up at the chief adoringly. *His bride*, I thought.

The chief grunted, his lips drawn down at the sides in a stern grimace. He studied Aunt Astrid, judging her.

Without saying a word, my aunt spoke with her hands. As she did, she conjured a cloud in front of her. Within the cloud, pictures began to form of wild horses running in open fields, of rushing rivers of crystal-clear water, of the hot springs steaming in the early morning, of tall grass with children running and laughing, and of Chief Big Running Fox's entire tribe peacefully living on this land as a full moon rose in a purple sky.

The chief watched the pictures, his eyes the only thing moving on his deeply etched face aside from the tears that had started to fall down his cheeks. The young woman standing next to him took his hand. They didn't speak. They didn't look at each other. But so much was said between them.

The Enisi began to whine and pointed at Aunt Astrid. But my aunt didn't move. She didn't even look at the shriveled-up, whining thing that was inching its way closer to her.

"We will stay!" The Enisi's voice was cracking.

But the chief was not looking at the Enisi. His eyes were fixed on the picture of his whole tribe together on this quiet, peaceful land.

Aunt Astrid showed him one last view. It was a beautiful grassy path with thick pine trees all around it. Wildflowers peeked from behind small rocks, and a lush, red fox stood proudly on the path. Pointing to the fox, Aunt Astrid urged the chief to follow it. With her ability to see beyond the dimensions, she knew that if he followed the fox, he would lead his people to the other side, to the next life, to peace.

The Enisi screamed. It was enough to make all of us cover our ears except the chief, who snapped his head in her direction, his eyes on fire. The Enisi immediately stopped her bellowing and cowered in front of him. His voice was low and gravelly. I could barely hear him, but what I did hear held so much authority that I was afraid to look up. Swallowing hard, I kept my gaze lowered, just in case.

The Enisi sounded like she was begging. Hysterical gibberish poured out of her, but the chief said nothing more. Instead, he reached down to the young woman at his side and, with one mighty yank, pulled her up onto the back of his horse, where she held on with one arm around his waist.

Then from the flames stepped another girl, younger but just as pretty as the first. She walked along the side of the horse, holding the woman's other hand.

That's her sister. They are the siblings that died.

The three began to walk into the picture, and the entire tribe followed, all except the three men that had been the wolves...and the Enisi.

The chief looked back at us. In the split second in which I met his eyes, I did not see his lips move, but I heard his voice in my head.

"So many years I've lived with hate and resentment. I blame myself for letting others chain me to my negativity so that I've forgotten about peace. If only I'd lived in peace while I was alive. Thank you for helping me remember."

In the blink of an eye, the chief and the two women vanished.

"Let's go, girls," Aunt Astrid said, breathing hard and sweating. She reached down to Bea, helping her to her feet.

"Bea, are you okay?" I asked, stroking her hand as I held it tightly in mine. She nodded, but her eyes still shone with tears.

"We need to hurry," Aunt Astrid said. "Whatever happens, don't turn around."

Bea and I looked at each other and then at Astrid. But we heard the Enisi behind us. She was rambling on in English and in her native tongue, words we didn't understand all jumbled together. Then we heard the wolves, their growls loud and fierce and merciless. The wind began to blow, and I hoped it would be loud enough to drown out the sounds I knew were coming. I wanted to look behind to make sure that the wolves were not sneaking up on us and that the Enisi hadn't convinced them to ambush us and rip out our throats.

But when she started screaming, her voice carrying toward us on that sudden breeze, I closed my eyes tightly and stumbled along the grass away from the carnage. Bea covered her ears. Aunt Astrid kept her head held high and her feet moving. Within seconds, we were nearly running back to the path we had followed to get to the clearing.

The screaming and the sound of tearing flesh finally stopped. When at last all was quiet, I turned and looked. I saw nothing. No fire. No wolves. No Enisi.

"Did they get there, Mom?" Bea asked, her voice choking just a little.

"Yes, I can see them there."

"What about the other things, you know, that were sneaking in and out of the doors the Enisi left open during this lunar hoo-haa thing Bea mentioned?"

"Well, the ritual is over. The Enisi is gone. The chief and his tribe have passed on to the next life. There are a few things that remain here, trapped, until they find another way back to where they came from—or hiding if they have some other plans, good, bad, or indifferent, in mind for themselves."

"Do you get the feeling anything bad is still around?" I looked around us nervously.

"Not anything we need to worry about just yet," she said, smiling.

"How about you?" I squeezed Bea's hand. She still had tears in her eyes.

"That woman had lost her mind. She had fallen

into a black pit of evil and liked it. It scares me that our power can be so intoxicating that one day we might just give in to it, to the temptation to use it for ourselves. I just don't get it."

"It's okay, Bea. She's gone. The door has been closed. I don't think any of her energy will be coming back any time soon." My aunt sounded like she had on so many nights when we were kids and a thunderstorm or a scary movie had gotten the best of us.

We walked back to the spa slowly and silently. What were they going to think of three women staggering in at this hour? Our clothes were dirty and wrinkled but not too badly. We could just say we got a little turned around out on the nature path trying to take in the phase of the moon but were fine. No one was hurt.

But as luck would have it, the front desk was occupied by one young blond fellow who was happily reading a book as we walked in. He barely looked up as the electric doors slipped shut behind us. A security guard gave us a nod and a slight smile, probably thinking we had slipped into town for happy hour and were just making it back a little the worse for wear. I didn't have it in me to correct him. I didn't even want to speak as my aunt and Bea led the way to the elevator.

Too tired to argue, I climbed on board the elevator and was happy that it did not produce a single rattle or bump to make me nervous. In fact, it seemed to run more smoothly than it had before.

"Do you guys feel the difference?"

"I was just thinking that," they said in unison.

"The air is lighter, the lights are brighter, the energy is positive. Yeah, that is much better. I wouldn't be surprised if business picks up after this," Bea said.

"Well, I'm going to sleep in my room tonight." I scratched my head and rubbed my neck. "I'd like a hot bath and some room service and some bad television until checkout time tomorrow."

"I'm so tired I'm skipping the bath until five minutes before checkout. Good night, girls." Aunt Astrid waved and let herself into her room.

Bea didn't say anything as she unlocked the door. When she looked at me, I could see she was feeling a little better. What that Enisi had shown her really bothered her. I had the feeling it might not have seemed so horrible to someone like Blake, who saw the darker side of life a lot, or even to me with my more cynical streak. But it was so bad for Bea because she was so good.

"You going to be okay?" I stood in the hall with

my hands on my hips. "If you'd like some company, I can stay with you. Crappy television can wait."

"No. I'm tired." She managed a smile.

"You know, I think that after this vacation you planned, we all could use a vacation. Thanks, Bea."

This time she did laugh. A few tears fell, and I understood why. But her laugh came from that deep-down place real laughs always come from.

"Yeah, thanks for thinking of me. You can bet I'll return the favor."

"No, don't. I can't believe we have to go back to work the day after tomorrow. I could sleep for a week."

"Well, checkout is at noon. I'll come get you at ten till."

"Deal."

I waved and made my way back to my room. It was cool inside because I had left the balcony door open. I didn't mind. I grabbed the late-night menu and the remote control for the television, clicked it on, and stretched out on the bed.

Before I knew it, I was waking up to the sound of chirping birds and the sight of the sun starting to rise. The sky was a beautiful, cloudless pink, and the bare branches of the trees scribbled across it like it was a page in a coloring book. Checkout wasn't until noon. With a loud sigh of relief, I pulled the comforter around me and went back to sleep. It was a peaceful, deep sleep with simple dreams of people I knew catching a train, eating cake, and redecorating the café, the usual nonsensical things that made up dreams.

The funny thing was that I saw Officer Tom Warner in my dream. What was he doing there? He was smiling that wonderful smile that showed off his dimples and made his eyes into crescent moons. He was just there, I guessed, checking up on me.

Now, had I told Bea I dreamt of Officer Warner, she would have quickly run for some tea leaves to read my future and done a palm check to make sure no blocks of energy might impair my judgment and prevent me from kissing him or agreeing to another date.

So when I woke up the second time that day, I kept the characters in my dream to myself. But I couldn't help wondering about the person who wasn't there. I had dreamed of Blake Samberg before, harmless scenes in which he came into the café or was at Bea's house watering the garden or polishing shoes. Dream stuff.

But he hadn't been in that dream. I would never say a word to anyone, but I was disappointed.

Clementine Hotel

❧❧❧

"**A**re you nervous?" Bea asked me as she looked over the newspaper spread out on the counter. It was a slow day, and we were all thankful for that. After our three-day "vacation" at the Muskox Serenity Spa and Retreat Center, we were all exhausted. I was a good bit better off than my two partners in crime.

Bea, after her direct exposure to the Enisi, had suffered a migraine for two and a half days and bad dreams for almost a week. She had been able to talk with Jake about it since his job lent itself to the darker side of humanity. He could understand Bea's feelings just as she could understand his fear after aiming his gun at Blake. (He had spilled the beans on that and my name hadn't come up, for which I was thankful.)

"I'm not speaking in front of thousands of people, Bea. No. I'm not nervous."

I looked at my cousin, who nodded, her eyebrows arched high into her forehead while she pretended to read the news. I didn't think she believed me.

Between her and Aunt Astrid sharing the days, my aunt in the morning and Bea at night, while I helped all day at the café, I felt like I was repeating myself all the time.

Tonight was special, though. Both of them were in, and my aunt, shuffling receipts at her favorite table for two, seemed to be a little better than she had been the past couple of days. She was giving me sneaky looks, too.

"What?"

"Nothing," Aunt Astrid replied in a sing-songy kind of way while looking over her shoulder at Bea.

"You two are up to something."

"Us?"

"Yeah. And the last time you guys put your heads together, you came up with the genius idea of visiting the Muskox Serenity Spa and House of Horrors, thank you." I folded my arms over my chest and gave them a *harummff* that made them laugh out loud.

"We were trying to help you." Bea chuckled. "How were we to know what was going to happen?"

"Does your psychic ability tell you nothing?" I asked my aunt, who shrugged.

We were quiet as the last two customers in the place finished their coffees. A young man reading a book and checking his watch, looking like he was killing time, sat at the far wall underneath the picture of the black cat that had been hanging there since the reconstruction after the fire.

A woman nursed an iced tea while she studied her iPad. She sat next to the window and barely looked up.

I was happy business was slow. Even though Bea and Aunt Astrid had borne the brunt of the cleansing, I was a little burnt out myself. It seemed like the universe was aware of that, because it gave us steady business, but even the morning rushes were calm and devoid of any drama.

Noticing a few crumbs on the back table, I took one of the rags from next to Bea and walked back there to quickly wipe them off. The bells over the front door jingled, making me jump and turn around slightly, losing my balance.

"Meow." Treacle slunk in and made a running leap onto the counter, where he found a spot right smack in the middle of the newspaper Bea was reading.

"Well, hello, handsome," Bea said, scratching my cat behind his ears.

I walked over to the counter and took a seat on the stool in front of Bea and leaned my head in. Treacle gave me a head-butt of affection and purred loudly.

"Bea was reading that paper," I told him.

"It feels so good to sit here. It crinkles and is noisy and mine."

"You're going to have to move. Let her finish and then I'll put you back." I scooped up the soft feline and held him close to me.

When I had finally come home after the vacation in hell, Treacle had jumped up into my arms as soon as I walked in the door. I had missed quite a bit of excitement, according to him.

A new puppy had been adopted at the yellow house with the black shutters a few doors down, one of those black-faced, curly-tailed beasts that breathed funny and barked constantly.

Treacle had inspected a couple of abandoned buildings in the rougher part of town and was sure that more than just mice hid in the walls. I didn't want to hear about it. I had had enough ghost chasing and paranormal cleansing to last me a good while.

And a surprise had waited for me at the back window. I'd carried the big ball of fur with me as I peeked out the window to find a big, fat, dead rat.

What a nice surprise! I was grossed out, but this was my favorite pet's way of saying "I love you." I'd rather have died than let him think I didn't appreciate it. He'd head-butted my chin then pushed himself out of my arms in order to take a seat on the floor and begin a long, arduous grooming session.

I had been happy to be home. For the first time in a long time, the walls of my house gave me great comfort. They weren't the scary, isolating barriers they had felt like just a few days ago. They were just my walls, decorated with pictures I had chosen or drawn myself. The whole place, as simple as it might have been, reflected me. I saw myself in everything around me and was happy.

On my first night back home, I'd stayed inside and eaten soup in front of the television while I drew some pictures.

If a stranger had stumbled across my sketchpad, they would have turned it over to the police and sworn that I was some kind of serial killer or at least covering for one. But expressing the feelings that are deep down can help a trauma victim heal.

With charcoal and pencil, I drew the monstrous astral spider that had affixed itself to me. I drew the Enisi, her face full of anger and insanity. I drew the wolves that ultimately tore her soul apart.

Those hours spent creating the images that scared me took away their power. I remembered wondering if I'd have trouble sleeping if I thought too hard about the elevator or the hot springs that had almost drowned me.

But I didn't. I'd slipped easily and peacefully into a deep slumber that left me feeling refreshed.

So I didn't mind carrying the load for Bea and Aunt Astrid. They needed to recuperate, too. It was the least I could do for all they had tried to do for me.

"Hey! Check this out!" Bea said, picking the newspaper up and looking at some tiny print. "Waldo Ferguson, age eighty-nine, was arrested Monday for the 1952 murder of Sadie McGill. When questioned, Ferguson confessed to strangling the victim in what was once the Clementine Hotel, located in what is now unincorporated Wonder Falls. Within hours of his arrest, Mr. Ferguson collapsed and died of a heart attack."

"Well, I'm surprised the authorities moved so quickly on an anonymous tip," Aunt Astrid said without looking up at either one of us.

I looked at her and shook my head no to answer her question.

Aunt Astrid had also been laid up for a couple of days. "I can't take a punch like I used to," she had said in between a chuckle and a sigh.

I didn't want to think about my aunt being old, because to me she wasn't old. Astrid Greenstone was just more mature than Bea and me, not old, not winding down. I couldn't imagine going through losing her right now. Jeez, it felt like I had just lost my mom the day before. Everyone else on the planet only loses their mom once, and that is bad enough. Losing my mom and then Aunt Astrid would be like losing my mom twice, something I just didn't want to dwell on.

"Did you stop in room 116 before we left?" To be honest, I had completely forgotten about poor Sadie McGill, the mistress of her sister's husband. I could tell by the look on my Aunt's face that she had felt sorry for Sadie. I couldn't help but feel the poor thing had been cursed with a low I.Q. and high libido. Plain, old-fashioned common sense could keep a girl out of her situation. But what did I know about love?

"I did. It was empty. Empty of everyone and everything."

"I'm glad." I was. What the heck kind of existence was it for a person living or dead to loiter around a hotel waiting for their true love to arrive? That sounded seedy even though I really didn't mean it to.

"Where do you think Ferguson ended up? With Sadie or her sister?" Bea tapped her chin, thinking.

"I don't think the universe will give him such a good choice. He'll have to make amends, and heaven only knows what that will entail."

Treacle was fussing in my arms, so I let him go. He went straight back to Bea and plopped down on the newspaper. She scratched him behind the ears again, and this time we let him stay.

"You know, you guys don't have to wait with me. I can lock the place up." I tugged at the V-neck of my dress, which I was sure was slipping open a little too far.

"Are you kidding?" Bea shouted.

"I wouldn't miss this for anything. No way am I leaving," Aunt Astrid stated loudly as well.

I let out a sigh.

"That's why I'm here. I need to know what is going on, too," Treacle piped up. I gave him a narrow-eyed glare.

"You, too, Treacle?"

"Meow."

Rolling my eyes, I went back to wiping down the tables. I was a little nervous. I was wearing a bright-red dress that, at the time I'd bought it, I had considered modest but still flattering. Now, as I kept looking at my reflection in the storefront window, I was starting to think I looked like the whore of Babylon.

"You look so pretty. You really should wear dresses more often," my aunt said.

"And that color is fantastic on you. Not everyone can get away with something so bright," Bea cheered for me.

"You don't think it's too bright?" I tugged at the sleeves and again adjusted the V-neck.

"No! No way!" Bea and Aunt Astrid chorused.

"You want to be noticed. You just wait and see all the heads that turn. He won't want to turn his back on you for a second for fear you'll be swept away by someone else," Aunt Astrid encouraged. "Now, do you need me to explain how things go on a date?"

"Are you kidding?"

"It's been, well, to say a long time would be an understatement. I just want to remind you that no means no, and if you like the guy, play hard to get. Run just fast enough that he breaks a sweat but not so fast he can't catch you."

"I should have said no. Not because I didn't want to go out but because it is inevitable he'll have to deal with you guys."

"We are the first line of defense, Cath." Bea flexed her muscles.

"Do you need me to explain the birds and the bees?" Aunt Astrid piped up.

"Bea, is your mother on some kind of medication I don't know about? Has she been drinking?"

My aunt was really enjoying herself. I hadn't seen her laugh so hard in a long time, and I wasn't sure what about her explaining the birds and bees was so funny. I found it a bit gross if I had to be honest.

When the door jingled, my heart leapt in my chest, and I nearly tripped over myself in the tiny heels I was wearing as I turned to see who was coming in.

Surprise Visit

❧

"I'm surprised you are still open. I am in dire need of a cappuccino. I'll also need a double-shot espresso to go," Darla Castellan said as she flipped her hair and reached her perfectly manicured nails into her purse to pull out her wallet.

Normally I would have been seething on the inside that she would show up here tonight of all nights, but something inside me had changed. I didn't look at Darla and instead concentrated out the window.

Could it be that I was getting over this high school drama with her? Could it be that maybe I was maturing, becoming more aware of myself and less concerned with the opinions of people around me? My last few experiences had certainly given me a reason to do a little soul searching.

"That will be six dollars, Darla," Bea said as she hustled behind the counter.

"Six dollars? Wow. Who do you think you are, Starbucks?" Darla griped as she took out some money. "I don't have anything smaller than a hundred." She put the money on the counter and pushed it with her long, dark-brown nails toward Bea as if she were afraid their fingers might touch if she handed Bea the money like a civilized person.

"I'll help you with that, Bea," I said, scooting behind the counter.

"Oh, no you won't," Bea protested. "I won't have you risk getting anything on your new dress. Go on. You're off the clock."

Darla had acted as if she didn't see me as usual. But as I turned, obeying Bea's command, I saw her eyes float up one side of me and down the other as she looked at my dress. She delivered no comment, no eye rolling, no nothing. I must have looked good or else a snide remark would have been too much for her to keep inside.

The door jingled again. I did trip a little as I saw Blake enter the café. He nodded politely to Bea and Aunt Astrid. I wanted to shrink into the corner, but one thing a red dress like this didn't allow me to do was not be noticed. Blake stopped and looked at me as if I were a ghost.

"There you are," Darla said in a low, purring kind of way, snapping Blake out of his trance. "I got you a double shot." She handed him the espresso Bea had made.

What the hell were these two doing here? What was Darla trying to prove, and why in the world, after everything he'd said to me at the spa, was Blake willing to go along with her? My gosh, I couldn't imagine wielding the kind of power over the opposite sex that Darla did. It was truly jaw dropping.

I turned my back and busied myself with things that wouldn't get my dress dirty. I rolled silverware, stacked bags for carry-out, and grabbed the broom to sweep up the little pieces of nothing that were on the floor.

I couldn't help but feel like I was being watched. Peeking over my shoulder, I saw Blake doing the same thing. He had taken a seat next to Darla, and rather than looking at her when she talked, he lifted his eyes from hers to meet mine.

It made me furious. I swept faster, determined to get all the invisible dust pookies off the floor before they could develop into a real dust pookie. This wasn't right.

I stepped into a dress and heels and all of a sudden I was worth taking a longer look at? Who did Detective Samberg think he was? So it was true that if I were more high maintenance, I would be more to his liking? What kind of a sick puppy liked women like that?

The truth was that I was a jeans-and-T-shirt kind of gal. I liked my hair pulled back, and sure, I loved to be pampered and wear lipstick and smell good all the time, but life had a way of preventing me from getting those things sometimes. Plus, who could throw away more than thirty dollars every two weeks on fake nails? I sure couldn't.

"I'll be right back," I heard Darla say as she stood up from the counter, thrust her chest out, and sucked her stomach in, making her backside curve. If she'd tried to shake it any more as she walked to the ladies' room, there would have been damage to our furniture.

Before she had the door closed, Blake was up and at my side.

"Hi, Cath," he said in his no-nonsense, just-the-facts-ma'am kind of way.

I looked up at him and folded my arms, not uttering a word.

"You look really nice. Do you have plans tonight?"

"No. I'm going home to do the laundry. What do you wear when you clean?" Okay, childish, yes, I knew. But his date was in the bathroom, and here he was only willing to talk to me when it was safe. Was he really that much of a wimp?

My thoughts kept spinning like a wheel, and not a match, not a lucky number, nothing was coming up that I could grab hold of and form into a coherent thought to speak.

Plus, as much as I wanted to just tell him off, he looked really nice too. He was wearing one of my favorite gray suits with spit-polished dark-brown wingtips. Something about the gray and brown colors together really looked classy.

He smelled really good, too, like he had just stepped out of the shower after using a nice, clean-smelling soap. Nothing fancy. His hair was slightly mussed from the little bit of breeze that kicked up every so often outside.

Without provocation, I imagined him in a flannel shirt and blue jeans with a day's worth of stubble on his face and thought I might just faint at the sight of such a rugged, handsome man. Then I remembered what he'd said, and it felt like my heart had been pierced.

"Why would you get dressed up to do your laundry?" he asked. I couldn't tell if he was just baiting me or if he really was that dumb.

Shaking my head, I just went back to sweeping.

"Can I talk to you for just a minute, Cath?"

"I don't really think that is a good idea."

He stood there for a second. The words were obviously taking a little longer to sink in.

"It's important."

"Your date is going to come out of the bathroom any minute," I said seriously. "I'm not sure if she's told you anything about me, but I'll give you fair warning she isn't going to be happy seeing you chatting me up. You may not want Darla Castellan on your bad side."

"I really need to talk to you. Can we meet somewhere, or maybe I could stop by your house?"

"Are you serious?" The words came out like laughter, but my expression held no joy. "After all the things you said to me in my hotel room?"

"What?"

"After making it very clear that you not only think I'm crazy but my whole family is crazy, now you actually think I'd let you into my home? Why would I ever do that?"

"Hotel room?"

"Yes, hotel room. At the spa? Don't play stupid

with me." I took a deep breath and felt my eyes begin to sting with tears of anger. "If you want to forget everything, that is up to you. But one day you're going to remember what happened in that Prestwick house, and then you're going to wish you had been nicer to me."

"I do remember what happened there. That is what I'd like to talk to you about."

"Since when?" My voice was raised but not enough to cause anyone to look at us.

"Since right after it happened."

"You are full of it, because you told me in my hotel room that…"

"What are you talking about, Cath? I was never in your hotel room."

Someone Like You

I stopped my arms from flailing and lowered my own voice as my eyes scrutinized every syllable that came out of Blake's mouth.

"You were. You came in and said...people who believed in witchcraft or anything like that should be locked up."

Blake stood there looking dopey and confused.

"You said that even Jake would back you up on this. That nothing happened at the Prestwick house."

"Cath, I'm telling you the truth that I don't even know what room you were staying in. I didn't see you anytime except when we were all standing outside and the fire trucks and ambulances had showed up and one time when you were talking with Jake."

I swallowed and stared into his eyes.

"I was never in your room, Cath. Never once."

I wanted to tell him I must have had a horrible dream. But it had been so real. He was there. He flipped through that little booklet of his. He had the same condescending way about him. I talked to him and told him to get out of my room when he insulted my family and me.

Was I losing my mind?

"If you weren't in my room, then who was? Someone was there, someone who looked and talked and acted just like you. No. You're trying to fool me now. Is this something you and Darla cooked up between the two of you? Wow. Mensa should be chasing you two geniuses down."

"Darla? She's got nothing to do with this."

"Sure." I nodded, feeling my blood boil and pound in my ears. Two weeks ago, I probably would have collapsed under the weight of the depressing situation of Blake and Darla. But even if it was tearing me up inside, I was not going to let him know it.

"Look, I don't know what you experienced at that place other than getting your nails done, but it wasn't just your normal spa."

"That's right. You don't know what I experienced

there." The image of the astral spider clinging to my back pushed tears to my eyes. I bit my tongue. I didn't want to risk ruining the makeup I had so carefully applied.

"Cath, I had to investigate the suicide of two sisters. That was bad enough. But other things happened there, and all I kept thinking about was where you were."

"I had nothing to do with those sisters or anything else that happened."

"Of course you didn't. But you are the only one who might understand."

I stood there pursing my eyebrows, so I looked mad. All I really wanted to do was take his hand and hold it in mine. Wasn't that silly? With all of the mysteries and creepy-crawlies and monsters under the bed, all I wanted to do was hold Blake's hand.

He looked toward the back where Darla had walked to the restroom then took a small step closer to me. He was so handsome and strong that my head was swirling like a kid told to *pick one* while they stand in front of a counter loaded with dozens of different candies.

"I wanted to tell you thank you."

I heard what Blake said but again couldn't look at him.

"For what?" I swallowed, but my mouth was dry. What could he possibly have to say to me now?

"For saving my life."

I wanted to cry.

"I can't explain anything that I saw there that night in Prestwick. I don't have the words. But I remember what you did. I saw it and...I felt it."

What was he getting at? Did he want to say something else? I felt myself leaning closer to him, but I couldn't look up from the floor. I didn't trust that I wouldn't make a fool of myself right there in front of everybody.

"Thank you, Cath. I would have died if you hadn't been there."

Why couldn't he have stayed a jerk? Why couldn't he have actually said those mean things in the hotel room and made this easier on me?

"Cath, I need someone to talk..."

The bells over the door caught my attention, making me peek around Blake's broad shoulders. I wasn't sure if my heart leapt or collapsed inside my chest.

"Hi!" I said, sounding more excited than I really was.

Officer Tom Warner stood in the door wearing a brown blazer, a clean, crisp button-down shirt, blue jeans, and cowboy boots. He was holding a bouquet. He looked amazing.

Like a real gentleman, he walked up to Bea and Aunt Astrid and shook their hands before turning to me.

"You look beautiful," he said, shaking his head and offering me the flowers.

I smiled and inhaled deeply. They were red roses with little bits of baby's breath and lovely green ferns.

"Wow. These are beautiful. I don't think I've gotten flowers since my high school prom," I joked nervously. I sounded like a dork. This was worse than awkward.

"Here, let me put those in water. We'll keep them at the café if that's okay?" Bea offered, and I nodded, handing her the pretty flowers.

"I'm ready to go," came the shrill, condescending voice of Darla, back from powdering her nose or sharpening her claws or whatever she had been doing. She stopped, and without looking, I could feel her sizing up Officer Warner. Blake wouldn't be enough now that she saw I was with Tom. However, I didn't hear Blake answer her or make a move.

"Officer, I almost didn't recognize you out of your

uniform. You clean up real nice," Aunt Astrid said, trying to keep the levity up in the room.

"Well, thank you, ma'am," Tom replied politely. "I wanted to make a good impression." His eyes twinkled and his dimples made their appearance, making me blush all over the place. I had to be as red as the dress I was wearing.

"I think you've accomplished that," Aunt Astrid continued, unashamed that she was embarrassing me.

"We better get going," I said, in a hurry to get out of the café for a whole host of reasons. "Heaven only knows what my aunt will say next. She's been drinking all afternoon. Don't listen to her."

Tom laughed out loud, said good evening to Bea and Aunt Astrid, and offered me his arm as he escorted me out the door. I looked back to see Blake was still just standing there. What was I doing? Did I want to go out on this date? Should I apologize and just run back and tell Blake he could talk to me? He could talk to me as long as he wanted to about anything he wanted to.

"So, do you have any place in mind you'd like to go, or can I surprise you?" Tom asked.

"Oh, you know, I'm not sure," I hemmed and

hawed. "I've not been on a date in a long while, and well, I'm just not sure what to do."

I sounded utterly flabbergasted and let out a sigh, shrugging.

"Well, neither have I. How about we just play it by ear."

That sounded nice.

We walked a few more steps down the sidewalk.

"How about a couple of burgers?"

My stomach grumbled happily. I hadn't eaten all day due to my nervous knots, and a couple of burgers sounded fantastic. I nodded.

"I know a great place just on the edge of town."

"Okay."

Again we were quiet until we got to his car. I should have known from the boots that it would be a pickup truck, a red one.

"This is nice," I said, envying the huge monster of a truck compared to my beat-up old Dodge Neon.

"You like it? I'm glad. Hey, there is something I've been meaning to ask you."

Oh no, here it comes. The question that was going to make me hop back out of this truck, slam the door, and head back to the café. I braced myself.

"When you said you were kind of a ghost hunter, were you being serious?"

My back straightened, and my claws began to come out.

"Yes."

"That is amazing." His face seemed to light up. "I don't want to make you talk shop or anything, but ghosts and paranormal, well, that's sort of a hobby of mine."

"Really?"

"Really. I'm just fascinated by it. I can't say I've ever seen anything that I could definitely say was a ghost or spooky-spook, but as a police officer, I've seen some things that made me leave all the lights on when I went to bed."

"A big, strong guy like you afraid of the dark?" I teased.

"Yeah, if it wasn't for my cat, I think I'd be wearing one of those jackets with the sleeves that tie around the back."

"Right?" I smiled. "I have a cat, too. Treacle. He is a black cat with green eyes."

"You don't let him out on Halloween, I hope."

"Of course not. People always want to get a black cat…"

"…to use for pretend rituals and stuff, yeah. We advise everyone during the fall to keep their pets close to home."

As much as I tried not to, I was starting to enjoy myself. We climbed into the truck, and some old-time country music was playing softly. A man with a sweet voice singing about heroes always being cowboys filled the cab, and Tom seemed to ask all the right questions and have all the right answers.

He wasn't hard to talk to. He didn't pick arguments. He laughed at my jokes, and I couldn't help but laugh at his.

I had forgotten what I had been so nervous about. I had forgotten everything. Almost everything.

About the Author

Harper Lin is the *USA TODAY* bestselling author of 6 cozy mystery series including *The Patisserie Mysteries* and *The Cape Bay Cafe Mysteries*.

When she's not reading or writing mysteries, she loves going to yoga classes, hiking, and hanging out with her family and friends.

www.HarperLin.com